MURDERS
ON THE TRAIL

His eyes darted nervously through the early dawn grayness at the three motionless bodies curled in sleep. The fat one was on his back, staring straight up. Harry and Case both faced away from him. Harry was facedown, as if breathing dirt. Gregg's backbone shivered as he crawled toward the fat one, his eyes darting quickly at the other two for the slightest sign of movement.

The fat one did not breathe. His eyes were open, pupils dilated. Gregg put an ear near his lips, then searched a wrist for some sign of a pulse. He looked at Harry, curled on his stomach, facedown. "Wake up, Harry!" he shouted. "Your partner didn't make it."

Harry remained motionless. Gregg crawled cautiously toward him keeping one eye on Case. "Wake up!" he shouted, grabbing Harry's shoulder and rolling him over. His breath caught involuntarily in his throat. "My God!" He gasped.

Harry's throat was slashed just above the adam's apple. The last expression he'd had when alive was frozen on his whiskered face. It was a grotesque look of sheer terror.

The knife Harry had held against Case's penis lay beside him, caked with blood. Gregg picked it up, then looked at Case, who was now leaning on one elbow aiming Gregg's pistol at him.

"You had a busy night," said Gregg.

We will send you a free catalog on request. Any titles not in your local bookstore can be purchased by mail. Send the price of the book plus 50¢ shipping charge to Tower Books, P.O. Box 511, Murray Hill Station, New York, N.Y. 10156-0511.

Titles currently in print are available for industrial and sales promotion at reduced rates. Address inquiries to Tower Publications, Inc., Two Park Avenue, New York, N.Y. 10016, Attention, Premium Sales Department.

GUNS
FROM
THE EAST

Dick Taylor

TOWER BOOKS   **NEW YORK CITY**

A TOWER BOOK

Published by

Tower Publications, Inc.
Two Park Avenue
New York, N.Y. 10016

GUNS
FROM
THE EAST

CHAPTER 1

It sounded like a man's scream, but it was so brief Gregg couldn't be certain. He pulled up and listened carefully, hearing only the breeze caressing the jagged rocks. Musta been a hawk after a ground squirrel, he decided, or a blue jay, or even a mountain lion. They all made sounds that sounded almost human sometimes. Wasn't a man though. There'd be more screams if it'd been a man.

He'd waited another minute, listening carefully, looking in all directions. Nobody took this old soldier trail anymore, climbing these rocky ridges. Even in the old days trappers took it only when looking for game and soldiers took it to keep out of sight. Nowadays everybody took the southern route, through Holmes Pass, following the railroad; everybody except Gregg, and maybe a few others like him, men who wanted for one reason or another to be alone, to think some things through.

It wasn't that Gregg was antisocial, or burdened with heavy problems. Far from it. His sandy-haired, rust-toned face smiled more often than it frowned and he didn't waste a lot of time carrying a long face over problems of the world that didn't concern him. He figured he was luckier 'n most. He'd come outa the war weighing a hundred and seventy-five pounds of pure bone and muscle, with no scars or diseases to bother him every time the weather took a bad turn. He didn't have to stay home and wallow in the misery and humiliation of defeat either. He had a favorite uncle in the Dakota Territory who'd offered him a chance to start a new life, in a new world—the West. He was a damn sight luckier 'n most. Gregg had read a lot about the West, from news stories in old issues of the *California Star* and *Alta California*, to the wild exaggerations in weekly magazines like *Wild West* and Frank Lesley's *Illustrated Weekly*. He'd also read some of the more humdrum but truthful memoirs of early trappers, traders, and prospectors. He'd liked what he'd read, and was eager to start a new life in the West.

But he didn't want to rush things. He wanted to spend a few days completely alone on the trail with memories of the past he was leaving behind. He wanted some time alone to say good-bye to his mother who had died of consumption the year he finished his schooling and to his father who had been killed in the war without even tasting the glory of dying in combat. A runaway team pulled a supply wagon over on him. He wanted to say good-bye to the small farm that had reverted to wilderness during the war and was sold for taxes before he could get it producing again. He wanted to recall happy faces of his youth that no longer walked this earth, or if they did, were no longer happy. He wanted to be alone to say these good-byes, to put that portion of his life behind him, for good.

It was not self-pity that he felt as he looked back. He drew strength and warmth from his past, not regret or tears. The three days he had spent alone on the trail had been three good days, three inspiring days, three peaceful days. It had been a long time since Gregg had had a chance to be alone with his own thoughts, his memories. He could use three more such days.

He'd hoped the sound he'd heard, like a scream, was an animal and not a man. He was not yet ready to be with people again.

All morning it had threatened rain, the sky was getting darker by the minute. Gregg got his poncho out of the tool box on the side of the wagon and crawled into it, tying it snug around his neck and pulling his hat on square. He'd be sweating in a few minutes, but that was better'n getting caught uncovered in a sudden downpour, then spending the rest of the day feeling like he'd come out of a swamp.

He took off his gun belt, rolled it up carefully in a canvas wrap, and stored it under his seat. He felt the need to have a gun handy, but a man could blow a hole in his leg drawing under a heavy poncho. Besides, he had his rifle on the seat beside him, and the small derringer he kept hidden in his waistband, under his vest.

A lotta people thought the .41 caliber pistol was fit only for a woman's hand, or maybe her garter belt. But Gregg had learned from a riverboat gambler that a small weapon, well hidden, sometimes provided more security than a buffalo rifle sitting out for all to see.

Skala, his sorrel Morgan horse, moved forward without an order the minute Gregg picked up the reins. She also stopped without an order when another scream ripped through the stillness, more clear this time, unmistakably human. It was a man in pain, a man hurting bad. Gregg started to grab his rifle, but it was awkward holding both it and the reins through his poncho. He merely leaned it on the seat beside him and snapped the reins for Skala to move on, around the sharp bend ahead. That man, whoever he was, wasn't far away.

Around the bend was a wide grassy plateau that caught Gregg by surprise. He'd been climbing for more than two miles, steady and steep. The flat plateau came sudden, and unexpected. There was about ten acres, flat as a table top. A large cottonwood tree spread out about a hundred feet ahead. Three men were around it, looking as surprised to see Gregg as he was to see them.

Actually, only two of the men were surprised. The third, spreadeagled to the tree, didn't notice. His shirt was ripped to shreds and bloodsoaked. His head hung limp to one side. He wasn't out, not yet. He still stood, or rather half stood and half leaned into the tree. But his eyes were glassy, like he had a weak grip on consciousness, if not on life itself.

Under the blood and dust that covered damn near

all of him were patches of a white silk shirt and expensive, fancy boots, the kind Gregg had seen riverboat gamblers wear.

The other two men, the ones dishing out the punishment, wore the drab, dust-caked cotton and denim of saddle tramps. They could have been settlers, miners, or any of the unwashed and unshaven that were streaming West. The one with the rifle aimed at Gregg's gut had a round, simple-looking face—not as hard and intense as the one who dropped the bullwhip and drew his pistol and started giving orders.

"Throw it down, mister," he said, nodding at Gregg's rifle.

Gregg cursed himself for not having kept the rifle in his hands, as he'd started to do, as he should have done. Now he faced two barrels, both aimed right at him and both within easy range. It was the same old story, more battles were lost through stupid mistakes than were won through brilliant strategy. Now he had no choice but to wait until they made a mistake, as big or bigger than the one he just made.

He smiled, spreading his hands in a gesture of peace. "I got no business here, gentlemen," he said. "With your permission I'll ride through, without stopping, looking back, or seeing a thing."

The hard-looking one picked up his whip, flipped it back expertly, and walked within reach of Gregg's eyeballs. "You better do what you're told," he growled.

Gregg lifted his rifle by the barrel and leaned over the side of the wagon, dropping it harmlessly to the ground.

"Now get down here," ordered the man with the whip. He was thin and wiry. There was a brown tobacco juice stain running down the side of his mouth.

Gregg stepped down, holding his hands high.

"What'll we do with him, Harry?" asked the fat one.

"Don't know yet. Keep an eye on 'im until I finish with Case here."

"You just about finished with Case haven't ya, Harry? A few more swings a that bull whip and he's a dead man." Even as the fat one talked to the one called Harry he kept a close eye on Gregg. He was taking no chances.

"I got a few things in store for Case before he dies," said Harry, chuckling. He glanced at Gregg impatiently. "What's your name, boy?"

"Gregg Martin."

"Where ya headed?"

"Riley."

"You any kin to Flem Martin?"

"He's my uncle."

"Folks say he's an Injun lover."

"I wouldn't know about that."

"I don't give a damn for Indian lovers."

"Never known any Indians myself."

Harry smiled. "I've tended to my share of 'em, just like I'm tending to Case Anders here."

Gregg's eyes scanned the five horses grazing at the edge of the flat. One was a piebald stallion, graceful and majestic—covered with the lather of a hard ride. The other four grazed apart, all bays and of inferior breeding, mustangs probably. Gregg figured the stallion belonged to the one getting the whipping. Harry and the fat one had brought the others, probably the end of a string of mounts they'd brought to ride the man down.

"What the hell we gonna do with him, Harry?" asked the fat one.

"You just keep an eye on him." Harry holstered his pistol and went to the tree, loosening one of the ropes holding Case, then flipping him around so his back was to the tree, and tied the rope again jerking it so Case's back was pulled into the bark. Case didn't make a sound, but his teeth flashed in a grimace when the bloody flesh of his back rubbed into the rough bark of the tree. His eyes were closed. His dark hair hung over his sweat-covered forehead. His face was clean shaven, but weathered. He didn't spend all his time at a poker table thought Gregg.

"You hearing me, Case?" asked Harry, slapping Case's cheek, but getting no response.

He was a big man, with a touch of gray in his well-trimmed sideburns. Gregg guessed he was in his early forties, vain in his appearance, like a gambler or a professional soldier, and tough as barbed wire to take the beating he'd taken without begging for mercy.

"You hearing me, Case?" asked Harry, slapping Case's cheek. He got no response.

Harry smiled. "You're hearing me all right," he said. He unbuttoned Case's pants, jerking them down to his knees, then ripped open his longjohns, exposing his genitals. He pulled out a knife.

"Feel this, Case?" asked Harry, holding the flat of the cold blade against Case's penis. Then he laughed a high-pitched, nasal laugh.

Gregg began to sweat under the poncho. Two streams of perspiration crawled from his armpits down his rib cage like ribbons of cold steel. He wasn't thinking of Case, but of himself. Harry might let him ride away from a whipping, but Gregg would never be allowed to witness a mutilation and then ride off to tell about it.

He glanced at the fat one, who was watching his every move, then looked at Harry. One of them had to make a mistake soon, very soon. And when they made it he had to be ready to move, instantly. If he didn't he was never going to make it to Riley, or even out of these hills.

"You've chased your last woman, Case," said Harry, reaching for Case's genitals. The instant he touched them the fat man's eyes opened wide. He couldn't wait to see the gore. "Git 'em, Harry!" he screamed, eyes gleaming with anticipation. "Git 'em!"

It was the mistake Gregg had been waiting for. As the fat one watched Harry, spellbound, Gregg's wrist moved quickly, flipping the small derringer free of his waistband, pausing for only an instant to aim from the waist, and firing. The sound, muffled by the poncho, was like a popgun. The bullet, however, was no toy. It blasted a two-inch hole in the poncho and smashed into the fat man's chest, just below the heart. Gregg leaped forward, stretching his arm for as wide a swing as he could make under the poncho and knocked the rifle free. Then he twirled, aiming the derringer at Harry. "Drop it!" he commanded.

Harry froze, glancing at the rifle knocked behind the tree, gripping his knife. "Now!" shouted Gregg.

Harry dropped the knife and held his hands high.

"I'm dying, Harry!" cried the fat man, lying on his back, clutching a bloody hole in his side, his eyes glazed with fear.

"You stupid bastard!" shouted Harry. "I told ya to

watch him!"

Case opened his eyes, a slight smile parting his lips. Gregg picked up the rifle and motioned Harry to sit down, near the fat one. He took Harry's pistol and then tied his wrists to his ankles. He cut Case free and eased him to the ground. "You all right?" he asked.

"I could be a damn sight worse," replied Case.

Gregg brought his wagon forward and unhitched Skala, feeling more warmth for her than for any of the men he now had in his command. He got a bag of salt out of the wagon and began rubbing it in Case's wounds.

"My God!" exclaimed Case, gritting his teeth from the burning pain.

"It'll make 'em heal faster," said Gregg.

"If I can survive the medicine!"

Gregg rubbed axle grease over the salt, which eased the burning a little.

"That son of a bitch took my woman!" said Harry bitterly. "He and his fancy clothes and slick words. He filled her head with a lot of shit and—"

Case chuckled. "You've said that so much you believe it yourself, don't you, Harry?"

"That's enough," interrupted Gregg. "Save your stories for the law."

"Law?" asked Harry. "What law you talking about?"

"There's bound to be law, even out here."

Harry laughed. "Let's see now, there's army law at Fort Collins, four days southwest ahere—if you don't run into some Indians before you get us there—and then there's regular law at Cheyenne. They even got a sheriff. But that's four days due west, also through some Indian country. There's a couple a railroad stops between here and there, but the only real law you'll find there comes from a shooting iron. Right now you're the only one that's got shooting irons, so that makes you the law."

Gregg paused, turning the picture over in his head. Any way he looked at it, it was bad.

"You gotta get this lead outa me, mister," moaned the fat man. "I'm gonna bleed to death if ya don't!"

Gregg examined the wound. It was swelling and turning red and blue. Blood came out in regular spurts. Gregg decided against probing for the bullet. It was too close to the heart. He'd seen more soldiers die from people probing for bullets than he had from wounds, particularly when the bullet was near a vital organ like the heart.

He put a bandage on it. "Hold it," he said. "The pressure will help stop the bleeding."

In a few minutes the fat man's fingers were seeped in blood. "I'm bleeding to death!" he moaned.

"Serves you right, you stupid bastard," snarled Harry.

At dusk Gregg shared some dried beef and pemmican with Harry. The fat one was too weak for food. Case had passed out, or else just fallen asleep. Gregg started to tie him up, to make sure he didn't wake up in the night and cause any trouble. But he took one look at Case's back and decided against it.

"He's a no-account son of a bitch," said Harry. "We had a good spread, me and Lorrain. We was gonna build a bigger cabin and I'd already marked off the land I aimed to break for spring planting. We was just about to get on our feet, when along he come and wrecks it all."

"Save it, Harry," said Gregg.

"No man's got a right to take another man's woman, no more'n he's got a right to steal a man's horse. A good woman's hard to find in this country."

Gregg was dog tired and he faced a lot of problems the next day. "Get some sleep, Harry. We're pulling out with the first light."

"I can't sleep hog-tied like this!" complained Harry. "I'll be up all night!"

Gregg frowned, looking hard into his eyes. "Shut up, Harry, before I tie a rope around your mouth."

Harry became very quiet. In five minutes he was snoring. The fat man groaned, pausing occasionally to emit a blubbering sound. None of it bothered Gregg. Three years of living with soldiers had accustomed him to the sounds of men sleeping, including the sounds of wounded men. He listened to the gurgling in the fat man's breathing and wondered if he'd make it through the night.

Then he wondered what he'd do with the three of them the next morning. Neither Case nor the fat one were in any condition to ride. They'd have to share the bed of his wagon. He'd have Harry ride ahead, where he could keep an eye on him. He couldn't travel far like that though. A man couldn't remain alert enough to keep an eye on the three of 'em around the clock—not for long. The fat one wouldn't be any trouble, but Harry would—and so would Case. Harry was hell-bent for sinking his knife into Case's privates, and Case would be just as determined to see that it didn't happen, which meant going after Harry first chance he had. A man in the middle of two animals like that didn't stand a chance if either one of 'em got the drop on him. Gregg pondered this until he fell asleep.

He was usually a heavy sleeper, waking up slow. During the war when he was scouting, or behind enemy lines, heavy sleep was a luxury he couldn't afford. But alone, as he'd been since leaving the train at St. Louis, he fell asleep quick and hard and enjoyed waking up slow, like the coming of daylight, not really getting full awake until he smelled coffee brewing.

This time his instincts were as raw as they'd been when patrolling behind enemy lines. The instant his eyes opened he was wide awake. All of his nerves and muscles gripped tight. It was the silence that he noticed first. He could hear nothing but his own breathing. It wasn't natural, that heavy silence.

His eyes darted nervously through the early dawn grayness at the three motionless bodies curled in sleep. The fat one was on his back, staring straight up. Harry and Case both faced away from him. Harry was facedown, as if breathing dirt. Gregg's backbone shivered as he crawled toward the fat one, his eyes darting quickly at the other two for the slightest sign of movement.

The fat one did not breathe. His eyes were open, pupils dilated. Gregg put an ear near his lips, then searched a wrist for some sign of a pulse. He looked at Harry, curled on his stomach, facedown. "Wake up, Harry!" he shouted. "Your partner didn't make it."

Harry remained motionless. Gregg crawled cautiously toward him keeping one eye on Case. "Wake up!" he shouted, grabbing Harry's shoulder and rolling him over. His breath caught involuntarily in his throat. "My God!" He gasped.

Harry's throat was slashed just above the Adam's apple. The last expression he'd had when alive was frozen on his whiskered face. It was a grotesque look of sheer terror.

The knife Harry had held against Case's penis lay beside him, caked with blood. Gregg picked it up, then looked at Case, who was now leaning on one elbow aiming Gregg's pistol at him.

"You had a busy night," said Gregg.

Case looked in his eyes, as if searching for something. Not finding it, he shrugged. "It was them or me."

Gregg nodded as Case continued to search his eyes, like a poker player looking for a signal. Gregg looked away, determined not to send one.

"Catch!" said Case.

Gregg looked up just in time to catch his pistol. "I got no quarrel with you," said Case.

Gregg nodded, holstered his weapon and started a fire. He rolled up his bedroll and stored it carefully on his wagon while the coffee boiled. He never looked at Case, nor did he turn his back on him. Case watched carefully as Gregg stripped the personal belongings from the two dead men, putting them in an empty flour sack. They didn't amount to much—a few coins, a pocket watch, two cheap rings. Harry had a ragged but new-looking photograph of himself and a woman, a rather attractive woman, standing solemn and straight. The name Clarence King, photographer, was stamped on the back. Gregg put it all in the sack then put it in the wagon and poured himself a cup of coffee.

"Help yourself," he said to Case, who remained motionless until it was offered. Case tried to get up, but grimaced from the sharp pain in his back. One of the clots ripped loose and a few drops of fresh blood appeared. He sat back down.

Gregg poured a cup and handed it to him.

"Thanks."

Gregg merely nodded. After he finished his coffee in silence, he began digging a pair of shallow graves. "I figure I spent half the war digging," he said, clenching his teeth. "It was either trenches or graves, or latrines or garbage dumps; swore I'd never do it again."

Case sipped his coffee slowly, blowing it occasionally. He didn't figure Gregg was trying to make conversation, he was just letting off steam with words. Case didn't reply except to say, "Good coffee."

When Gregg finished digging he leaned back, straightening out the kinks, then pulled the two bodies into the shallow graves, scraped the sandy soil and rocks over them, then used their saddles for headstones. He bowed his head, mumbled something Case couldn't hear, and remained silent a few seconds. Suddenly his head lifted, he helped himself to more coffee and poured Case a refill.

"Who were they?" he asked, wiping beads of sweat from his forehead with a swipe of his forefinger.

"I only knew 'em as Harry and Clyde. Couple a homesteaders."

"Never saw a filthier pair. Did they ever bathe?"

"Not unless they had to. They been dogging my trail for weeks. Finally they got a string of ponies and just kept riding and switching mounts until they run me down. I shoulda bushwacked 'em days ago, but I kept figuring they'd give up and head back to where they belong."

"Where's that?"

"Dennis Valley, couple a days' ride south of Denver."

"Pretty far from home."

"Yep."

"Musta wanted yer ass pretty bad to go to so much trouble."

"They did."

"What do you plan to tell the law?"

Case's eyes flicked open, surprised like. "The law?"

"You just killed a man, maybe two for all I know."

"It was a personal matter."

Gregg thought it was a weird joke until he realized Case was serious.

"This is the West," explained Case. "This country is full of the remains of men who died about the same way these two did, except there wasn't always somebody to bury 'em and say words over 'em. They just laid where they dropped until the buzzards ate their flesh, the sun bleached their bones, and the wind returned their dust to dust. The law don't stick its nose into those things. No need to."

"Then just what the hell is the law for in this country?"

"When a man kills to gain something that isn't his—money or property or a reputation he don't deserve—then it's the law's business. But the law isn't interested in things like this. This was personal, between Harry and me. He figured he had good reason to come gunning for me. I figured he didn't. I won. He's buried and that ends it."

Gregg felt a strange sense of relief. The night before he'd been worried about traveling with two wounded men and an animal who wanted one of them dead. Only moments ago his head was swirling with vague fears of an investigation of two killings, one of which he probably caused. Images of lawmen and attorneys and judges, and a jury swirled through his head. With the images came a frustrated sense of uncertainty, apprehension. What if the jury was filled with friends of the two dead men? Would they believe him, a stranger?

Suddenly all the worry went away, wiped clean by Case's confident shrug and authoritative pronouncement of "That ends it!"

Gregg hitched up Skala and got ready to move out. Case remained motionless, and silent. "Can you ride?" asked Gregg finally.

"I need to heal some first."

"Where ya headed?"

Case shrugged. "Any railhead, new mining town, cattle shipping point—anywhere fresh money's flowing."

"House dealer?"

"Not when I get my own stake."

"You should have somebody take care of that back. They cut you up pretty bad."

"It'll be all right in a few days."

"You're welcome to stretch out in the wagon bed if you like. I'll drop you at the first ranch that'll take ya in."

Case grinned. "That sounds better'n sitting here." He slowly got up and walked to the rear of the wagon. Gregg took out the tailgate and Case crawled in, snakelike. He took it slow and easy and managed to get all the way in without breaking loose another scab.

Suddenly Case started laughing.

"What's so funny?" asked Gregg, replacing the tailgate.

"I just thought of Lorrain, the one in the picture you took off a Harry. It's his wife."

"What about her?"

"She came to me in tears, just to get away from him for a while. She wouldn't leave him because of the ranch. She loved that ranch if only Dirty Harry wasn't there. She always called him Dirty Harry."

"Well, she should be one happy lady now."

"Yeah. Funny how things work out sometimes."

"You sound like you've just done the world a favor."

Case chuckled. "That's just how I feel!"

It was then that Gregg first noticed Case's gun and holster.

It was the enlarged grips that caught his eye, the kind Gregg had used in the war. Like many cavalrymen, Gregg started the war with a pair of pistols, a saber, and a carbine. In the midst of battle that gave him twelve rounds of firepower for certain, a carbine that could only be used effectively as a club or a saber that didn't have the reach of a foot soldier's bayonet. He quickly traded the bulky saber and carbine for an extra pair of .44 colts, which he kept strapped to his saddle. Then he had twenty-four shots, which was a lot of firepower at close quarters. He used enlarged grips to reduce recoil.

Case saw him eye the pistol and took it out of the holster, breaking open the cylinder. "I ran out of ammo," he said, showing Gregg the empty chambers. "That's why they were able to jump me."

"What happened to the front sight?"

"I saw a front sight hang on a man's holster once," he said. "Filed mine off the next day." Case slid the smooth-barreled gun into his holster easy, "I'd feel a hell of a lot safer if I had some cartridges," he said. "A man feels half naked with an empty gun."

Gregg tugged on the reins for Skala to move out. "In weather like this it don't hurt a man to be half naked," he said.

CHAPTER 2

LaVida Tyson was about to come apart, and no one knew it better than LaVida Tyson. For weeks now she had been holding everything inside, feeling the pressure grow, dreading the spark that would set her off. It would happen any day now. She knew because she no longer dreaded it. She yearned for it.

A lot of people thought LaVida had a good case of cabin fever, a common ailment among women living on isolated ranches, miles from the nearest neighbor. But that wasn't her problem. LaVida was a well-organized, hard-working self-starter who took pride in managing her household efficiently and properly. She didn't need swarms of people around. All she needed was her work and her man.

She had once had that, when she and Bert first

moved to the one-room log-and-sod cabin in the middle of the vast, flat valley. There was just the two of them in those days and the blue-gray mountains just before sunrise, mountains that changed color every hour until the final rays of the sun gave them a pinkish tinge before turning dark for the long, silent evening. For company there were the sounds of the livestock and the sweet smell of spring drifting through the small window. That seemed like another life now, way back when Bert's ambition made him look like a dashing young knight in shining armor in her youthful eyes. That was before she realized what ambition could do to a man, before she saw what it did to Bert.

The log-and-sod cabin was gone now, replaced by a crisp white ranch house that sprawled seventy feet across the front, with a large kitchen in the back and a dining room big enough to serve twenty people comfortably. Each of the servants' quarters behind the house were larger than the old log-and-sod house had been. It was a different world now, LaVida's private world, or private prison, filled with a cook and two house servants and a daily routine of supervising household chores, reading the few periodicals that came her way, and putting a cap on the rage that erupted within with more and more frequency.

The long narrow bunkhouse, down near the stable and corral, constituted still another world, one filled with strangers who kept their distance in sullen silence and familiar faces that looked at her with distrust or pity or both. LaVida was uncomfortable with distrust and their pity made her furious.

Jamie McPherson dominated the world around the

bunkhouse. When Bert was gone, which was most of the time now, he left Jamie in charge and Jamie never missed an opportunity to let LaVida know that he, and he alone, was boss of the ranch. There was nothing LaVida could do but accept it, along with Jamie's strutting, arrogant ways. There were invisible but clearly understood lines drawn between their individual worlds. Neither crossed the line without clear and urgent reason.

But the overbearing weight pressing LaVida was not an absent husband, an arrogant young ranch foreman, or the isolation. It was time; time dripping away unused, time wasted. LaVida would soon be considered old. Her coal-black hair and smooth creamy complexion, hints of her Indian ancestry, still had the sheen of youth. Her blue eyes, a gift to her bloodline from a French trapper two generations back, and her handsome body, built like her German father, were alert and quick. Still, she would be forty soon, and in the young West, forty was old.

LaVida bitterly resented this. Never in her life had she felt more vigorous, more able, more filled with a passion for life. Yet in the eyes of those who dominated the young country, she would soon be considered old. Every empty, eventless day that crept away left her feeling more and more cheated.

Jamie McPherson and his ever present sidekick, Lew Rollins, galloped into LaVida's world, crossing the line that she guarded carefully. Although still in her long flannel nightgown, she quickly strapped a wide leather belt around her waist to convert it into a house dress and stepped outside to intercept him before he got to the front porch.

"A couple of strangers are heading this way," announced Jamie, dismounting several yards from the house. He was tall and slender and moved with the confidence of command, though he was careful not to intrude too far into her world. Jamie knew where his authority ended. Lew, wide-shouldered and heavy in the gut, remained mounted, well behind Jamie.

"What do they want?" asked LaVida suspiciously.

"I figured maybe you knew."

"I'm not expecting company."

Jamie smiled, his thin lips curling downward. "Then I'll handle 'em." He started to mount up.

"We'll see what they want," said LaVida, her jaw set.

Jamie paused, as if challenged. He looked at Lew, then back at LaVida, whose jaw was determined. "Okay, if that's what you want. But I'll be close by, if there's trouble."

Gregg Martin walked his Morgan to the ranch house, keeping the wagon going as smoothly as possible. New scabs on Case's back stretched and gave way every time the wagon swayed too much, or hit a bump too hard. "Morning, ma'am," he said, removing his hat.

"What happened to him?" asked Jamie, eyeing Case.

"It was a private matter," replied Gregg, taking an immediate dislike to Jamie's superior air.

Jamie examined Case's fancy boots. "A gambler, eh?"

"Could be. Who's asking?"

"Got caught cheating at cards I bet. Probably had it coming."

Gregg felt offended, as if he and Case had gone through a battle together and were now bound by the shared experience. He came down from the wagon in one leap, fists clenched.

"Now you two colts hold your vinegar," ordered Case. He had struggled to prop himself on an elbow, aiming his pistol at first one of the young men and then the other. "I'm sure this lady has better things to do than watch you two draw blood to prove you're a man." He looked at LaVida. "I could sure use a fresh drink of water, ma'am," he smiled.

"We tend cattle on this ranch, not dogwhipped tinhorns," sneered Jamie. He started to say more, then saw Case's gun trained right between his eyeballs and decided against it.

LaVida's eyes froze on Case. "There is water, and food, and a bandage for those wounds."

"I don't want to be that much trouble, ma'am."

"It's no trouble."

Jamie looked furious. "Now just wait a goddamned minute here!" he shouted. "No tinhorn's gonna—"

LaVida continued looking directly into Case's eyes. "Shut up, Jamie," she said simply, so simply and with such confidence its impact was devastating. Jamie's eyes flared. He looked again at Case's gun and twirled his horse around, galloping off.

Gregg looked relieved. "Damn it, Case," he said. "What if he'd noticed all the empty chambers in that gun."

Case gave a carefree tilt to his head, still smiling at LaVida. "When bluffing it's best not to think about the lousy cards you're holding," he replied. His head suddenly slumped forward in complete unconsciousness.

LaVida leaped into action, signaling two servants to help get Case into the house, ignoring Gregg who watched in awe.

"Get a pan of warm water and towels," ordered LaVida. As one servant disappeared she turned to the other. "Make a poultice with ivy leaves soaked in vinegar. Hurry!"

Case was put on a clean bed, on his stomach. LaVida pulled off his boots, then eased off his tattered shirt, examining his wounds without flinching. She touched his forehead with a small, delicate hand. "Has he had this fever long?" she asked.

"It started this morning. He had chills later. Now the fever's back."

"We must treat it first."

She loosened Case's belt and peeled down his pants, exposing soft white buttocks that contrasted sharply with the raw red meat on his back and the dark hair on his thighs. As she examined his back more closely her hand rested on the white of his buttocks which she unconsciously rubbed as if fondling a baby's skin. Her pink tongue slid over her upper lip, making it glisten in the soft light. Her breath began to become deeper. "Is he a gambler?" she asked softly.

"Yes ma'am." Gregg was torn between a respect for her maturity and a fascination with the grace and beauty of her movements.

Her eyes roamed hungrily over the length of Case's long, rugged nakedness. "Gambling had nothing to do with this. They shoot crooked gamblers, or else lynch 'em."

Gregg had the feeling she was talking to something

within herself. He felt no need to reply.

"It was a woman," added LaVida knowingly. She ran her hand through Case's dark grayish hair, turning his face slightly toward her to study his profile. "That woman knew exactly what she was about, too," she added, again knowingly.

The servants came with the water and the poultice. LaVida cleaned his back quickly, expertly, then very gently covered the wounds with the poultice. Her hands moved with skill and confidence, but her eyes remained wide, excited. Her breathing became more and more intense. It was as if she were struggling with both his wounds and some inner wound within herself, a wound that became more and more inflamed every time her hand brushed across the soft whiteness of his skin. Before she completed dressing his back she was panting as deeply as if in a foot race.

Gregg watched spellbound, feeling the tension grow in her. He still felt useless, but he made no move to leave. There was something about the way she touched and looked at Case's helpless body that convinced him a fire was growing inside her. He felt the heat of the fire.

She finished covering Case's back and waved the servants out, standing motionless until the door was closed and the three of them were alone and the silence of the room was broken only by her deep breathing as her small hand ran up Case's thigh to his buttocks and then down the other side.

LaVida loosed the leather belt around her nightgown and let it fall to the floor, then leaned forward, touching her lips to Case's soft white skin. "Do you have any idea what I feel right now?" she asked.

"Yes," replied Gregg softly.

"I can't hold it in any longer."

"Don't try."

She pulled the gown over her head, dropping it on the floor, then leaned still further over Case, running the nipples of her bare breasts across the crease in his buttocks and down his thighs. Again she kissed his flesh, running her tongue back and forth. "Please," she said softly. "Please!"

LaVida went to the foot of the bed, standing with legs spread, gripping a heavy bedpost. Her eyes never left Case's flesh as she leaned forward, resting her chin on a fist gripping the bedpost. "Please," she said once again.

Gregg stood behind her and dropped his pants. He took her hand, guiding it to his rising staff. She fondled it fervently, then gently, until it completely filled her hand and grew hard. She guided the head between her legs. "Now!" she exclaimed. "Now!!"

Gregg eased into her, surprised at her moist receptiveness, surprised and delighted. He entered as easily as dipping a bolt into a grease bucket. He started moving slowly in and out, but LaVida would have no part of that. She squirmed backwards, anxiously, "Faster! Faster!" she pleaded. "Please, please! Faster!"

Gregg lunged forward again, and again, picking up speed until beads of sweat began collecting on his forehead.

"That's it!" exclaimed LaVida. "That's hitting it!" For a brief exhilarating moment she threw her head back in ecstasy, closing her eyes and sucking air through gritted teeth. "Oh, my God!" she screamed.

Gregg's knees almost buckled when he exploded inside her, his sperm gushing out with such sudden force it oozed from around his throbbing shaft and ran down the inside of her legs.

LaVida leaned her head against the bedpost and remained perfectly still a moment after Gregg withdrew and pulled up his pants. "You're good," she said softly. "Very good."

"It takes two to tango."

She stood straight, walking back to Case's side. She placed her hand on his flesh, her eyes once again glistening. "I'll take good care of your friend," she said.

"No question in my mind about that," replied Gregg, backing out of the room on tiptoe. She was about the most hungry woman he'd ever seen. He closed the door behind him and left the house, perfectly confident Case was in good hands.

He rode less than a mile, carefree and happy, when Jamie and Lew Rollins rode up behind him. Lew just sat on his horse, like a huge lump of silent flesh waiting to be told what to do. Jamie pranced back and forth beside and around Gregg's wagon, restlessly displaying the spirit of both himself and his mount. "Is that tinhorn your kin?" he asked.

"Hardly."

"What's he to you then?"

"Just a friend."

"You make a habit of picking up mangy dogs that's been whipped?"

Jamie, obviously spoiling for a fight, used an intimidating tone of voice. Gregg wanted to meet the challenge, but he knew he'd never get a fair fight with nobody but Lew watching. He decided to curb his anger, for the moment at least. LaVida had left him feeling so at ease with the world it wasn't hard.

"If you have business with me, come out with it," he said. "If not, you're holding me up."

"I just want to warn you. Bert Tyson won't take it lightly if he finds some tinhorn has taken up with his wife."

"You're warning the wrong man, aren't you?"

Jamie sneered at Gregg's gray Confederate pants. "You and the tinhorn made me look bad back there—real bad. I won't be forgetting it—Reb."

Gregg merely nodded, holding his tongue. He snapped the reins. Skala leaped forward.

"We'll meet again!" shouted Jamie, scowling.

CHAPTER 3

Bert Tyson decided to skip the afternoon session. He had to ride to Marble Creek and keep those two saddle tramps in line, or else they'd drift off. They'd been there three days and Bert wasn't sure they'd wait any longer. The only reason they'd waited this long was because Bert threatened to ride 'em down if they left.

Bert Tyson was one of those large men who made people feel his size as well as see it. He was tall and broad shouldered and he had large hands and feet. His mouth was wide and his eyes bugged out of his head like on a bull frog. He'd told those two drifters to stay put for three days and they were afraid to do differently, afraid of Bert Tyson. But the three days were up now and they were more restless than they were scared. Bert wasn't at all sure he could hold 'em in line any longer.

Mr. Kassner followed him out of the ornate boardroom into the wide hall leading to the kitchen. Kassner only had a moment. Louis Whisler, of Whisler, Stocken, and Jeffers, was about to give his report on eastern industrial investments and Kassner wanted to hear every word of it.

"You can stall them one more day, can't you?" he asked nervously.

"I'll try, Mr. Kassner. They're getting damned restless though."

"Offer them more money."

"They've got too much now. It's burning a hole in their pockets!"

"We'll give them a decision tomorrow, for sure."

"That's what I told them three days ago. Tomorrow don't seem to ever come."

"This is a very complicated matter, Bert."

"They don't know that."

"There's no necessity in their knowing that. Just stall them one more day. It's very important."

"How long you plan to keep the board in session?"

"We should wind it up in the morning."

Bert Tyson looked relieved. "Good." If he'd had to sit through one more dry report on investments he knew he'd go loco.

Kassner snapped his riding crop crisply against his shiny leather boot before making a brisk about face and marching back to the boardroom, his boots making accented clicks on the hardwood floor. He was a head shorter than Tyson's six feet three inches and tried to make up for it by wearing high-heeled boots and always holding himself rigidly erect. He still had to look up to see Tyson's eyes, which made him uncomfortable. The only time he really enjoyed talking to Bert Tyson was when they were seated in his study. There, Kassner's chair was elevated and he towered over anybody else seated in the room.

Bert went to the kitchen, looking for Shelly. He'd get back from Marble Creek shortly after dark and he planned to have a get-together with her. She'd put him off the previous night, claiming to be too busy in the kitchen, preparing food for members of the board. She wasn't going to put him off again.

They were a good pair, he and Shelly. She would never have the job running Kassner's ranch house if it wasn't for him, and he'd never be able to stand it through Kassner's annual meeting with his board of directors if it wasn't for Shelly. Without her he'd go loco with those stuffed shirts.

The annual meeting was held in early summer in the massive home Kassner had built on his ranch in the Dakota Territory, a three-hour carriage ride out of Riley. He built the house to live in, but after one harsh winter his wife insisted that they move to San Francisco. Now he used the ranch home for the board meetings and for short visits during the summer and early fall.

His board members came from both coasts in one of the railroad cars built by the newly formed Pullman Company. At Cheyenne they boarded Kassner's private car for the northwest journey to Riley, where horse-drawn carriages waited to conclude their trip.

All were dutifully impressed with the beautiful blue-gray hills surrounding the ranch, as well as the sense of oneness they felt with nature in the isolated setting.

But in spite of their many "Ohs!" and "Ahs!" all were only too happy when the board meeting ended and they were back in their respective urban settings. Blue skies did not really look as pretty to them as coal smoke. There were no profits to be made in blue skies.

Kassner insisted that Bert Tyson sit in on most of the meetings, particularly those that promised to bring up problems that couldn't be solved using normal business methods. If Tyson's services were to be utilized in solving certain difficult problems, Kassner wanted the entire board to share the responsibility in making the decision to use them.

He knew the board resented Tyson's presence in so many of their meetings. They viewed him as some kind of animal Kassner kept on a leash. Kassner shared their view, of course. Tyson was some kind of animal. But he was needed, and Kassner wanted his board to be constantly aware of that need.

Tyson knew how the board felt about him, but it didn't bother him because he also knew how dependent they were on him. He once said to Shelly, "They remind me of little boys who have attended a very exclusive school where they've learned all there is to know about manners, dress, and business. About the only thing they didn't learn was how to find their ass with a corn cob."

Shelly wasn't in the kitchen. Tyson frowned and headed for the guest houses. She was probably doing some maid's work again instead of supervising, as she was supposed to do. Two cooks and several maids had been hired just for the annual meeting. There were more than enough hands to do all the work. But Shelly was in charge and she frequently did a lot of it herself, just to make sure it was done right. Tyson found her in one of the guest houses, helping Dora, her daughter, make a bed.

People were frequently surprised to learn Shelly and Dora were mother and daughter, they looked so different. Dora, almost seventeen, was taller than her mother, and slender. She had small breasts and dark hair and her skin became heavily tanned in the summer and was still dark in the early spring. Shelly was fair and her hair had been very blond in her youth. Now she was in her mid-thirties and it was beginning to get darker. She had more breasts than any man could ask for.

Both had pretty faces, but Dora's features were more delicate.

In spite of their differences, they had a similar sense of rhythm to their movements. When making the bed they moved together gracefully, like two dancers who sensed each other's next move.

Because of Shelly, Dora had never known fear or want or hunger or cold, or any of the things Shelly had never really been without.

Because of Dora, Shelly had never for a moment considered quitting or running, no matter how tough things got. There had been times when she had nothing in the world but Dora. But that had been enough to keep her going.

Bert stood in the opened cabin door a moment, watching them move silently together. Dora noticed him first and frowned, which irritated Bert. There was no reason for her to resent him like she did. "I wanta see you tonight, Shelly," he said. It sounded like an order, which made Dora frown even more. There was another difference between Dora and her mother. When Bert gave an order, fear came to Shelly's eyes. Hatred came to Dora's.

"I won't be long," Shelly said to her daughter, then walked outside the cabin out of earshot.

"Must you talk like that in front of Dora?"

"She knows what's going on."

Shelly looked up into Bert's eyes, then glanced down. "I've been thinking about us, Bert," she said. "It's not right, living like we do."

"It's a little late for that kind of thinking."

"It's not right, Bert! You have a wife and—"

"Was living on the line right? You want to go back to that?"

"I'll never go back to that."

His eyes hardened. "What are you trying to say, Shelly?"

"That it's over between us, Bert. I don't want to see you any more."

Bert grinned like a man holding a full house against two pair. "Just what do you plan to do, Shelly?"

"The same thing I'm doing now, except—"

Bert slowly shook his head, his eyes getting harder, his confident grin remaining unchanged. He didn't need to use words.

Shelly's eyes opened wide. Bert loved to see that. If there was anything he loved to see in a woman more than big breasts it was big eyes, filled with fear, fear of him.

"Mr. Kassner says we do good work here, Dora and I. He told me so himself!"

"Mr. Kassner doesn't do the hiring, Shelly. Mr. Kassner doesn't want to be bothered with those little details, that's why he turned them over to me."

Shelly stared at his hard eyes only a moment, then her gaze fell to the ground.

"I'll see you tonight!" he stated, and left. When he walked past the cabin Dora was standing in the window, looking at him. She looked taller somehow, more mature. Bert's attention became fixed on her eyes, staring hard at him.

There was neither fear nor weakness in her eyes. There was only determination and the most fierce hatred Bert Tyson had ever seen in a pair of eyes.

He kept feeling the sting of Dora's eyes as he saddled his horse and headed south toward Marble Creek. Her anger burned into him like a pair of redhot branding irons. It wasn't her anger that bothered him though. It was her complete lack of fear. Dora had been sheltered from life by her mother, sheltered and protected to the point that she didn't know fear. He would have to do something about that. He was convinced she would be a constant burr in his saddle unless he put a little fear in her craw.

He saw smoke from a campfire ahead and began shouting. "Howdy, boys! It's me, Bert Tyson. I brought you a little something for your dinner!"

He kept shouting until he was certain they knew it was him. They were an edgy pair of young bucks, as apt to shoot as ask questions.

They kept a filthy camp, with half empty tins scattered around soiled clothes hanging over rocks, bedrolls looking like somebody'd just stepped out of them. The two young men were whiskered and dirty and when Tyson dismounted he could even smell them. They reminded him of a couple of bear cubs that had been holed up for the winter and were coming out mean and lean and filthy.

Jim was the taller of the two, and the brighter. He stood like a piece of well-worn rope. Danny was shorter and heavier—and meaner. Bert had never seen Danny's stained front teeth when they weren't clenched with hate.

Tyson took a bottle out of his saddlebag and tossed it to Jim. "Thought you boys might be getting dry," he said.

Jim held the bottle at his side and just stared at Tyson. "When do we ride outa here?" he asked.

"I'll know tomorrow."

"You been saying that for three days!"

"You're being paid well. You'll have another fifty to split tomorrow, just for sitting on your ass and drinking that whiskey."

Danny clenched his teeth and his fists. He bounced back and forth on the balls of his feet, like a high spirited horse about to break loose. "Tell 'em, Jim!" he shouted.

"Now hold on, Danny," said Bert.

"Tell 'em, goddamn it! Tell 'em or I'll tell 'em!" shouted Danny.

Jim walked close to Tyson and spoke in a low whisper. "One more night here, with nothing but some whiskey, and he'll go beserk," he said.

"Don't the money mean nothing to him?"

"You gotta understand, he just drifted in from Yuma—Yuma prison. He's wound up like a bolt of lightning. If I so much as raise my voice I'm afraid he'll explode. Another day is no good, Bert. I gotta get him outa here, tonight!"

Bert rubbed his wide jaw, looking just under the brim of his hat at Danny, still rocking back and forth on the balls of his feet, his fists and teeth clenched, his eyes wide and wild. Bert Tyson could feel what was going on inside him. As a younger man, he'd been that tight himself, many times. His paw had tried to beat it out of him when he was just a boy, but the beatings just made it worse, like Yuma prison had made it worse for Danny. There was only one thing that would drain off all that piss and vinegar.

Bert looked at the bottle he'd handed Jim. "That do you till morning?" he asked.

Jim smiled. "This and the money I'm making for just sitting."

Bert nodded, then turned to Danny. "How'd you like to spend the night at the ranch?" he asked. "Get yourself a hot bath, some hot grub."

Danny sneered. "How about a hot woman?"

"That too."

"You wouldn't be afooling me, would you?"

Bert laughed, slapping him on the shoulder. "Saddle up!"

Danny frowned. "I'll have a chunk a yer hide if you're fooling me, Bert, a big chunk!"

"We're wasting time, boy, saddle up!"

Jim opened the bottle and downed a long swig. "Hey, Danny, ya wanta borrow my lucky piece?"

Danny grabbed his crotch. "Here's all the lucky piece I need!"

"What lucky piece you talking about?" asked Bert.

Jim pulled out a highly polished brass cartridge and pitched it up, catching it, then pitched it up again. "It's never failed me yet!" he said.

"You polish it enough," said Danny. "You keep your lucky piece. Bert's got what I want." He let out a loud yell that spooked the horses for a moment. It even spooked Jim.

"Hey, you made me drop my lucky piece," said Jim, dropping down on all fours to start searching.

Danny and Bert climbed into their saddles and headed for the ranch.

Jim kept searching in the grass, making a wider and wider circle as he raked his fingers to the soil. "Damn it, Danny. If you've made me lose that I . . ." his voice trailed off as he dug in the grass.

It was well past dark when Bert and Danny got back to the ranch. The full moon was bright enough to cast shadows around the big house and the cabins scattered around it. The tight clump of cabins in a semicircle immediately behind the big house were where the directors were staying. None of them were lighted. The directors were still meeting in the board-room with Kassner.

There were lights in only the one cabin, somewhat removed from the others.

"Is that where she's at?" asked Danny impatiently.

"That's it," replied Bert. "Remember now, wait until you see her mother come to my place. Then make your move."

"Yeah. Yeah!"

"She may be a little wild at first."

Danny's eyes glistened. "The wilder the better!"

Bert left Danny in the shadow of the stables and headed for his cabin, across from the one Shelly and Dora used. He put a lamp in the window to signal Shelly he was ready for her. She'd delay a bit, just to be ornery. But she'd come. Shelly wasn't like her daughter, headstrong and independent. Maybe she had been when she was Dora's age, but not anymore. Life had drained it all out of Shelly, gotten her used to having a bit in her mouth. It only took a little dig of the spur to remind Shelly who was boss.

He smiled to himself. Danny was gonna be good for Dora. He'd put the spurs to her all right. With all the piss and vinegar he had inside; she wouldn't be so damned independent after Danny got through with her. And what the hell, it wasn't as if Bert were throwing some helpless young virgin to a stud bull. It wouldn't be Dora's first time. He'd seen her himself, down on the creek bank with that Poulson boy. There were probably others too. The way Bert figured it, when Dora reached the age to be curious about it, she tried it. Women who grow up around horses and whores don't make a big to-do about things like that.

But she might not take to Danny. She might just balk on him. That could be dangerous.

If she raised too much of a ruckus, enough to interrupt Mr. Kassner and the board, there might be hell to pay—what with her mother in Bert's bed and Danny being nothing more than a saddle tramp. Kassner didn't have much patience with the problems of the hired help. He might just run her mother and her off the place and call the sheriff to haul Danny away, just to quiet things down and to set an example to the rest of the help. Kassner was great on setting examples.

Dora was too smart to let something like that happen. She wouldn't cause a ruckus.

But then again, she might. A man can't always tell what a girl like her will do. He'd better not take any chances.

Bert took off his gunbelt and hung it over a chair, then got down his rifle and loaded it—something he rarely did inside the house.

The country was full of drifters these days—men who would steal the shirt off your back, men who would kill for a meal, or the touch of a woman. Nobody would pay much attention if Bert killed one of them attacking one of the girls on the place. It would be a hell of a lot simpler to handle things that way, if Dora lost her head and got spooked, than to try to make up a pack of lies for Kassner and the board.

He'd sure hate for anything to happen to Danny. Jim would have to pick up a new sidekick to handle the Flem Martin job, and that might take a few days. Besides, Danny was as good with a pistol as could be found anywhere, and it's always good to have a man on a job that's good with a pistol. But if worse came to worse, if Dora balked and caused a big ruckus, the best thing all around would be for Danny to get killed. Then nobody'd have to explain anything.

Bert leaned his rifle against the window sill. He'd just have to keep an eye peeled until he knew Danny was inside Dora's cabin, and there was no noise.

When Shelly arrived she didn't notice the guns. She didn't notice anything. She just walked silently to the bedroom, her eyes down, and began undressing in the dark.

Bert continued staring out the window. He saw Danny dart nervously out of the shadows and knock on the front door of Dora's cabin. Bert reached for his rifle.

"You coming or not?" asked Shelly, crawling nude

under the sheets, anxious to get it over with.

"What's your hurry? There's no other customers waiting," said Bert.

"Very funny."

Bert cocked his rifle, Danny was bouncing on the balls of his feet, speaking anxiously into the closed door. Suddenly the door opened, just slightly. Danny's shoulder lunged into it busting it wide open. He disappeared inside. Bert held his breath and waited. The light went out. There was no noise. Bert smiled. He waited a quiet moment, then clicked the cartridge out of the firing chamber and returned his rifle to the wall. "How about a drink?" he asked.

"Make it stiff."

Bert got a bottle and two glasses and walked into the bedroom. As his eyes grew accustomed to the darkness, Shelly's fair body gleamed alluringly from the white sheets. She was sitting up, fondling her drink, her large breasts hanging like delicious fruit. He quickly stripped and crawled in bed, trying not to feel irked over Shelly's annoying habit of keeping her eyes down or looking the other way when he stood before her nude. He didn't expect applause, but looking the other way every time made him feel repulsive, like he was something dirty that she preferred not to see.

He reached for her breasts. He had never seen a pair of breasts that excited him like Shelly's did. They had a certain firm roundness that was unmatched, and the nipples were warm and comfortable in his mouth. He sometimes tasted sweetness when kissing them. He liked to run the tip of his tongue around one until it grew hard and then try to see how much breast he could get in his mouth. There was always a lot left over.

After running his tongue around the nipple he felt his cock begin to rise. He tilted his head up and on impulse of passion kissed her lips. Shelly immediately jerked her head to one side.

"Goddamn you, Shelly!"

"Whores don't kiss customers. You know that."

Bert went completely limp. "Goddamn you!" he shouted angrily.

She sat up, glaring at him fiercely. "You're really something, Bert, you know that? You scare the shit out of me, threaten my job, and expect me to love you for it. You want a whore at your beck and call? Okay, you've got a whore at your beck and call. You want to fuck? We'll fuck. You want a blow job—you'll get a blow job. You live up to your part of this deal and I'll live up to mine, being the whore we both know I am. But don't look for extras, Bert, not any more. You burned all that out of me long ago, with fear and your big fists and your bullying ways. You probably burned it out of LaVida the same way."

"Leave her out of this!"

Shelly laughed. "Does it bother you to hear a whore use your wife's name?"

Bert was not only limp, but completely frustrated. Nothing was going the way he had expected. He rolled over and reached for a cigar and a glass of whiskey.

They remained silent a long, tense moment. Finally Shelly leaned over and cradled his soft penis in her hand. "Poor baby," she said, pressing her lips to its smooth head. Above and beyond her fear of Bert, sometimes of her hatred of Bert, she had a deep respect for his cock. She loved to feel it grow in her mouth, giving her a sense of worth and power, and when the mood between them was right she could get it up time and time again, and when they finally fell asleep, exhausted, she slept with the satisfaction of knowing it would rise again at the mere touch of her tongue the next morning. Bert's cock made her feel alive and worthy and needed—and it stilled all desires between her legs.

But the mood was all wrong tonight. Even the head seemed to soften at her touch, to shrivel and recede from her lips. "Poor baby," she said again.

Bert gulped down his whiskey, jammed his cigar out and turned his back to her. "You fucking whore!" he shouted.

"Poor baby," murmured Shelly softly.

As Bert's ears grew accustomed to the silence he could hear the creaking of the hardwood floor, the whir of a slight wind cutting around the corners of the cabin, the screech of an owl. Had his ears been a little more sensitive, or perhaps if he had just concentrated, he might have heard the muffled cry from Dora's darkened cabin, and the pained whimpering that followed.

CHAPTER 4

The final item of business to come before the board was the Flem Martin matter. It had originally been scheduled first because Kassner considered it the most important thing the board would discuss. But at the last moment Kassner moved it to last to give Wes Darby time to pay Flem a visit.

Kassner sat at the end of the long oak conference table. Wes Darby, his eyes twinkling as they always did when he was about to spin a yarn, sat at the opposite end. The eight directors sat on each side of the table in between. Bert Tyson, looking rested from a good night's sleep, sat against the wall, separate from the others.

Dora came in with a pot of coffee, refilling cups. Tyson didn't want more coffee, but he held his cup forward anyhow, staring hard at her as she poured. She gave him an equally hard stare then turned and quietly left the room.

There had been no fear in her eyes. None at all. Tyson had never seen such a headstrong girl.

Kassner called the morning meeting to order, making no effort to hide his nervous excitement. There was a bright gleam in his eyes, a slight nervous twitch around the corners of his lips, an extra stiffness in his erect posture.

"Gentlemen," he said, as if announcing the final event, the big item of business everybody had been waiting for. "Senator Clayton has an announcement of interest."

U.S. Senator William S. Clayton looked unsmilingly around the table. He had the portly look that was popular among men of influence. Dark hair tumbled in thick globs from his head and face.

"Gentlemen," he began. "Very soon now the Congress of the United States will vote to establish the Wyoming Territory. President Grant will appoint a Territorial Governor. All of us on this board know what that means, and how urgent it is that our own Felix Kassner receive that appointment. It is essential not only for our business interests gentlemen, but for the welfare of the people of this great Territory."

The Senator paused while there was a polite round of applause.

Tyson almost laughed when he saw the agitated excitement in Kassner's eyes. He couldn't understand how anybody could get so excited over being appointed territorial governor.

"There is one slight problem," added the Senator

gravely. "The President feels that the man he appoints must have the support of the majority of the people of Wyoming. Mr. Kassner, of course, has such support, as all of us know. But there are always those few bitter souls who will go to any extreme to convince the President otherwise. I am referring, of course, to Flem Martin, publisher of the *Riley Gazette.*

"As much as I would like, I will refrain from giving my full and complete opinion of Mr. Martin and the sinister forces he represents. Suffice it to say that he can present a problem of major proportions if he opposes the appointment of Mr. Kassner, as he most surely will, unless we take steps to stop him—drastic steps if necessary."

Kassner's eyes were almost frantic as they swept the table. "It's inconceivable to me that one newspaper could exercise the power you suggest, Senator," he said, his voice cracking with emotion. "Can't you tell the President the truth and . . ."

"Those in Washington who do not know the real facts might be led to believe that this newspaper speaks the truth," replied the Senator.

Kassner just shook his head, his eyes glazed. Tyson wanted to ask what the hell difference it made who got appointed governor. The damn job wouldn't pay anything and there weren't a hell of a lot a governor could do. But he didn't dare. It was obvious that to Kassner the appointment was a matter of life and death.

The next man to address the board was Wes Darby. Tyson had warned Kassner about Wes Darby, but to no avail. Well, they'd all find out now. Wes Darby was just like Flem Martin. They were peas from the same pod and there was no way in hell Kassner was gonna hire one to turn on the other. No way in hell. But Kassner had to try it. He'd try anything to be governor. Anything at all.

Darby had spent his whole adult life roaming the West as a printer, reporter, editor, and finally a newspaper publisher. He'd known the early trappers and traders and prospectors. He'd lived with the Indians, before they began turning on the white man. He'd known the whores and the gamblers and the kids who started punching cattle with stars in their eyes and he'd seen them grow old quick as their legs bent from being in a saddle too long and their feet got to where they hobbled unless they were in a stirrup. He'd seen the stars fade from their eyes but they kept right on punching cattle, because they weren't fit for anything else.

Darby knew those people, as few others knew them. He also knew western newspapermen, better'n any living soul.

He knew them because he'd been one of 'em. He knew Flem Martin, inside out.

Kassner might know a lot about investing money and managing business affairs, but Tyson was convinced he displayed a real ignorance of men, particularly western men, when he figured he could hire Wes Darby to help put Flem Martin in line. Tyson tried to tell him. Well, now he'd see. The whole board would see. Some way, somehow, Wes Darby would walk out with his fat fee and a gleam in his eye. And Kassner Enterprises would get a kick in the ass. They'd see.

Wes Darby had a full head of snow white hair, impeccably combed. He had red streaks in his nose, a reminder of years of hard drinking, and pale blue eyes that were crystal clear and still full of life. Wes Darby bragged that in all his seventy-two years he'd seen much more in life to laugh at than fret over, and he'd done a lot of laughing.

"Mr. Kassner hired me to see if I could buy off Flem Martin," he began, with an impish smile.

Several directors chuckled, until they saw Kassner's face turn red. "Now see here, Mr. Darby!" Kassner shouted. "I made no such arrangement with you!"

Darby's impish smile remained undaunted. "Pardon me, gentlemen," he said. "Buy off are my words, not Mr. Kassner's. As I recall, he asked me to negotiate a business arrangement with my friend Flem."

"We won't bicker over words," snapped Kassner. "Please continue."

"Well, I explained to Flem as best I could that our kind of newspapering is a thing of the past now and he should do what I did—sell out and rest a spell. What the hell, I said, we've spent our whole lives fighting railroads, politicians, and barbed wire and now that the West is full of all three it's time we stop fighting 'em and join 'em."

Several of the directors chuckled, in spite of Kassner's stern stare. Wes Darby was a natural born ham and a story teller.

"I told him you gentlemen would pay him a damn sight more than his paper was worth, enough for him to live right high on the hog for the remainder of his days. But I'm sorry to report, he just wouldn't accept the proposition. You see, Flem's only sixty. He's not ready to stop yet."

"The man's a fool!" shouted Senator Clayton.

"He's an obstinate old bastard!" shouted another director.

Others mumbled similar obscenities, until Kassner stood and rapped the meeting to order. "Do any of you have questions for Mr. Darby?" he asked.

"Has Martin got a family? Maybe we can approach them," said Wisner.

Wes chuckled, which meant he was about to spin a yarn for an answer. "He had a wife once, even had a little piece of land he said he was gonna farm. Nobody figured it would last though. I remember he complained about that woman from the very beginning. She wouldn't bring in the wood, even after he chopped it, and she refused to get up first and start a fire. The thing that ended it was the time Flem was fitting a new stock for his rifle when his team hitched in front got spooked and jerked loose. He told her to go fetch 'em, but she refused. She said the grass was too frosty. Flem marched right straight to the back and dumped their supply of flour and sugar to the old sow. That was his way of telling her how he felt about things. Then he packed his belongings and went out looking for another newspaper job. He never tried marriage or farming again."

"Did they have any children?"

"Naw. Folks say Flem sired a few here and there, but none of 'em carry his name or have any claim on him. He's got a nephew back East. All the rest of his family is dead."

"How about his advertisers?" asked the banker. "Can we get to them?"

"Only two kinds run ads in Flem's paper—them

that have to advertise, even if it means supporting the devil hisself, and them that thinks like Flem."

"How could anybody think like Flem Martin?" asked Kassner. "He's against all progress!"

Wes Darby's eyes twinkled. "Men like Flem don't consider themselves opposed to progress, Mr. Kassner. They look at it like they are for a kind of freedom. The farmer puts up a fence and calls it progress. Flem Martin says that fence restricts folks' freedom to use the land. You gentlemen build railroads and call it progress. Flem Martin said you made ants and slaves out of the men you brought in to build it and that it brought in guns that killed all the buffalo and barbed wire that enslaved the land itself. He don't call that progress."

"Flem Martin would have anarchy!"

"Maybe so. A lota old timers in this country don't look at it that way though."

"Gentlemen! Gentlemen!" interrupted Kassner rapping the table. "This is all very interesting, but it's not solving our problem. Does anyone have any more questions of Mr. Darby?"

Silence.

"If not, we won't take any more of Mr. Darby's time. Thank you for being with us."

Wes Darby left the boardroom, climbed into his waiting carriage with a check for his consultant fee, and smiled all the way to the Gazette building in Riley, just like Bert Tyson had predicted.

"Well, gentlemen," said Kassner. "Any ideas?" The room became so quiet that when the floor creaked it sounded like lightning.

Bert Tyson had leaned his chair back against the

wall during Darby's presentation. He brought it forward, resting his two feet solidly on the floor. The moment he had been waiting for during the past three days had arrived.

"This is a grave problem that must be solved, gentlemen," said Kassner. "I'll ask one last time, do any of you have any ideas?"

The silence lingered for an unbearable length of time. Finally Kassner looked at Bert Tyson.

"Do you think you can handle this matter, Mr. Tyson?" he asked.

"Yes, sir."

Kassner eyed each member of the board. "I move that the matter of Flem Martin be turned over to Mr. Tyson, to be handled as he thinks appropriate. Do I hear a second?"

Senator Clayton nodded. "Second," he mumbled.

"Would all those in favor please raise their right hand," requested Kassner.

Every head in the room went down. Every hand went up.

"Thank you, gentlemen," said Kassner. "It's been a most productive and profitable session. This annual meeting of the board of directors of Kassner Enterprises is adjourned."

Tyson remained seated while the board members filed silently out to waiting carriages. He did not embarrass them by going out front with Kassner to see them off. Later he joined Kassner in the study, where the little man was so excited he could hardly contain himself.

"This was the most important board meeting I've ever called," he said, bouncing on the balls of his feet, his beady eyes once again getting that wild gleam of excitement.

"Looks like Kassner Enterprises will have another profitable year," replied Tyson.

"That's not what makes this meeting so important," snapped Kassner.

"Then what does?"

Kassner's eyes leaped on him, his teeth gritted with intense determination. "You have received the most important assignment of your life!" he stated. "The course of history may be changed as a result of your success!"

Tyson couldn't believe his ears, or more importantly, his eyes. "You mean Flem Martin—"

Kassner's rage exploded. "That man must be silenced!" he screamed.

Tyson left the board room scratching his head thinking Kassner had to be completely loco. He went straight to his cabin where Danny was bent over a plate of grub.

"The board voted to do it." said Tyson. "Get Jim and get going!"

Danny was furious. "I ain't going nowhere until I get even with that—"

Tyson backhanded him across the face, knocking him out of the chair. "You're gonna do what I say!"

Danny looked up at the big man and rubbed the red spot on his face. "Did you ever get your balls busted by the toe of a woman's boot?"

"No, and no woman ever drawed my own gun on me either. But what's done is done and you got work to do now."

"I'm gonna get her, Bert! No woman's gonna treat

me like that and get away with it!"

"You're not gonna get anybody until you finish the job I hired you for!"

"Gimme my gun."

"Just as soon as you're saddled up and aimed toward Marble Creek."

"All right. But as soon as that job's done I'm coming back. I'm gonna show that little bitch a thing or two!"

"Just make sure you get the job done, Danny. I don't want any gunplay if you can avoid it. But that newspaper must be wiped off the face of the earth!"

"Don't worry. I'll take care of the newspaper."

Bert walked Danny to his horse, waited until he was in the saddle, then handed him the pistol Dora had given him just before the morning session began. "I'll be watching until you're over the rise," he said.

"Keep watching long enough and you'll see me coming back."

CHAPTER 5

Gregg had seen enough western towns to describe one blindfolded. He fully expected Riley to fall into the same pattern of masculine slovenliness in the haphazard arrangement of buildings, the false pride in the fake storefronts, and most of all, in the impermanence of everything. Western towns looked like all the residents were on the verge of pulling up stakes and moving out. To a southerner accustomed to the dignity and charm of colonial architecture and the majestic permanence of glazed brick, a western town appeared dull, drab, and expendable.

Riley was a surprise, like a rainbow after a long gray storm. Gregg couldn't put his finger on it at first because Main Street had the same saloons and false fronts and was just as dusty as the other western towns he'd seen. But there the resemblance stopped. The boardwalk down each side of Main Street was not only clean but it was a good six inches off the ground, plenty high for a lady's long skirt to avoid dust in the summer and mud during the rainy season. The majority of houses on the side streets looked fresh and clean and had picket fences around them. Many were freshly painted. Colorful flower gardens were a common sight. There was a newly constructed church and a freshly painted one-room building with a flag on top of it and a bell on a tall post. It had to be the school. The depot was painted a bright red and the boardwalk around it was freshly scrubbed.

Riley was obviously a town where the people were bent on staying, with pride in their town.

The First National Bank was the most imposing building in town, filling a corner lot. Beside it was a smallish clapboard covered building with the word GAZETTE painted in large black letters across the entire false front. Gregg climbed down from his wagon and stretched his tired muscles.

He tied Skala to a hitching post and went inside.

The front office was small, with a narrow counter and a wall just behind it that hid the composing room and the mysterious happenings of the printing business. The office was empty and even though a bell jangled when he opened the door and jangled again when he closed it, nobody appeared.

"Hello!" shouted Gregg. He opened and closed the door again, jangling the bell.

A man in his middle fifties, with a handlebar mustache, thick glasses, and an ink-stained smock stuck his head from around the edge of the wall. "Want to place a notice?" he asked.

"A what?"

"An announcement! An advertisement!"

"I'm Gregg Martin, Flem Martin's nephew. Is he here?"

The man with the handlebar mustache stared at him a moment, looking from his eyes down to his boots then back up to his eyes. If he was impressed by anything other than Gregg's towering size he hid it well. "Not much likeness," he said.

"I favor my mother's side of the family."

"My name's Bellevue. I been with your uncle since he came to Riley, almost ten years ago."

"Bellevue what?"

He frowned. "Just Bellevue!"

"Would you mind telling my uncle I'm here?"

"He's over at Ryan's saloon. Better hurry if you want to talk to him. He's with Wes Darby."

"What's that supposed to mean?"

"You never heard of Wes Darby?"

"No."

"A friend of your uncle's."

"Why should I hurry?"

" 'Cause they'll be drunk by sunset and won't have anything to do with you, or anybody else for that matter."

"The sun's practically set now!"

"That's why you better hurry."

Gregg decided to get Skala bedded down first so he headed for the livery stable, then checked in at the hotel. By the time he got to Ryan's saloon dusk had eased over the town and Harry Pratt, the bartender, was busy trimming wicks and adding fuel oil to the lamps. Harry usually tended the lamps first thing in the morning, after sweeping up, but he'd spent the morning building two flower boxes for his home and he'd opened the saloon later than usual. He'd been behind ever since. He'd probably be behind again tomorrow too because he wasn't going to open the saloon until he'd painted both flower boxes.

Flem Martin and Wes Darby were at a corner table farthest from the door, sharing a bottle and squinting at a sheet of paper Flem had been writing on. "Hey, Harry! Bring us a lamp," shouted Flem.

Harry lit one lamp and carefully placed it on the wall stand behind their table. He wouldn't light the other lamps until it got darker. No sense wasting fuel oil.

Wes Darby laughed in his drink. "Put despised in there instead of hated," he said. "Despised has more of a sophisticated bite to it."

"I don't write for a sophisticated audience, Wes. My readers prefer the word *hate.* It socks 'em right in the gut."

"Remember now, Flem you ain't writing this piece for your unwashed readers working the ranches and businesses around here. You're writing it to send to Washington. You're writing it for Felix Kassner and his snot-nosed board of directors. Despised. That's the word that'll grab those people by the ass. Go on, put *despised* in there."

"Maybe you're right." Flem squinted as he made the correction with a dark fat pencil, then took a gulp of whiskey and read aloud. "Feared by many and despised by all."

"That's the stuff!" said Wes gleefully.

Flem made another correction, then read aloud again. "Feared by many, despised by most, and hated by everybody," he read, smiling broadly. It finally read like he wanted it.

They were enjoying themselves so much Gregg hesitated to interrupt. He recognized his uncle's long nose and prominent forehead, having seen him on several occasions as a youth. His body seemed more bent now, but it was still long and slender, just as Gregg remembered. It didn't surprise him that his uncle didn't recognize him. Flem Martin had merely added a few wrinkles and gotten gray since they'd last met. Gregg had grown up.

"I'm Gregg," he said, extending his hand. "You haven't changed much, Uncle Flem."

Flem Martin's face exploded into a beaming smile. "Well I'll be damned!" He stood up and clasped Gregg's hand, then pulled him to him and gave him a bear hug. "Well I'll be damned," he repeated, studying Gregg closely as if he couldn't believe the huge young man was really the tad of a nephew he hadn't seen in fifteen years. "You musta been no more'n twelve when we last met," he said.

" 'Bout that."

"This is Wes Darby, one of the best newspapermen to ever wield a type stick."

"Yer uncle's been drinking a little," said Wes. "Pay him no never mind."

"What are you two writing?" asked Gregg.

"Lead editorial for the next issue of the *Gazette*," replied Flem. "I'm calling it an Ode to Felix Kassner."

"What I just heard sounded a little bilious."

"Just a little bilious, you say?" Flem looked at his

old friend. "We better do a rewrite, Wes. We gotta make it a lot more bilious!"

"He only heard the lead. Read him all of it."

Flem started to read but was interrupted by a young boy who ran in the front door. "Mr. Martin, Miss Colburn said to remind you of the meeting tonight."

"What meeting?"

"The Better Riley Committee." The boy couldn't have been more than ten.

"Oh yeah. Thanks for reminding me, sonny."

"She said you promised to attend."

"You better go on home now. You're a bit young to be hanging around saloons."

"The meeting starts at seven, Mr. Martin."

"I know when it starts!" snapped Flem.

"She said to remind you."

"You've reminded me! You're a good boy, a fine boy. Now go away."

"It's six-thirty now, Mr. Martin."

"I can tell time, thank you!"

"She said you'd probably cuss a little, being reminded."

"I haven't cussed, goddamn it! Now go way, you little runt!"

"Yes, sir." The child backed toward the door.

"Miss Colburn is our local schoolteacher," Flem explained. "A delightful lady, delightful. Bright too. I never knew a brighter one. She could sit down here and help us write this editorial. Fit right in, she would. Damn shame they don't let women like her in a saloon."

The boy stopped at the door. "Miss Colburn's

counting on you to be there this time, Mr. Martin," he shouted, then ran out before Flem could scream a reply.

"That boy reminds me of a little stray dog that used to bark every time he saw me," said Flem. "I trained my horse to kick at his head. Damned mongrel dodged every time."

"Finish reading the editorial," said Wes, pouring himself another drink.

"Don't try to sneak ahead of me," said Flem pouring a drink for himself.

"Go on, read it," insisted Wes.

Flem squinted. "You're feared by many, despised by most, and hated by everybody."

"Beautiful, absolutely beautiful!"

"Your entire business career has been one of merciless rapacity. You fastened yourself on the vitals of Riley like a hyena, and woe to him who challenged you over a single morsel of your helpless prey."

"I hope this Felix Kassner has a sense of humor," said Gregg.

"Quiet, my boy," said Wes. "You're having the rare privilege of witnessing a creative genius at work, first hand. Go on, Flem."

Flem gestured as he continued, "You cast honor, honesty, and the commonest civilities aside in your frantic quest for wealth and power."

"Great stuff, Flem. You're in top form!"

Both men had to pause to drink to that.

Flem signaled Gregg to sit between them. He put his hand on his nephew's shoulder and looked him straight in the eye. "You know what I'm gonna do for you, boy?" he said.

"No."

"I'm gonna make a newspaperman outa you, that's what!"

"Finish reading the editorial, Flem," said Wes.

"I'm gonna start you out as a printer, my boy. You know anything about setting type?"

"I'm afraid not," replied Gregg.

"Teach ya myself. Have ya setting a thousand ems an hour—in no time, no time at all. Don't expect no favors though. You'll get sixty-five cents a thousand, just like everybody else."

"Big mistake, making a printer out of him," said Wes. "He'll learn his trade and walk out on you. Never saw a printer yet that didn't have itchy feet."

"You're right. I'll start him as a reporter. No drinking before noon."

" 'At's the stuff!" agreed Wes.

"That'll be the rule, hard and fast. Can't drink and write."

Gregg sat patiently while they spent a half hour deciding his career, pausing every few minutes to toast something or other, or to tell a story about some newspaperman they had known years ago. Seven o'clock came and went, as did eight. Gregg thoroughly enjoyed listening to the two men, even though they thoroughly ignored him as they reminisced over old times. He wondered if his uncle would ever get around to reading him the rest of the editorial.

When the bottle went dry Wes signaled Harry to bring another. "Hold it," said Flem, suddenly sober. "We gotta guard the press, remember?"

"Oh yeah," nodded Wes. "Damn near forgot the press."

"Whata ya mean, guard the press?" asked Gregg.

"Just a precaution, my boy. Don't bother yourself over it."

"Don't bother myself over what?"

Wes smiled. "See how nosy he is!" he exclaimed. "He's a natural born newsman, Flem. A natural born! I bet he can be an obnoxious bastard when he puts his mind to it."

Flem looked very serious. "I'm glad you decided to join me, my boy. We'll make a great team. You'll see."

"Aren't you going to tell me why you want to guard the press? Guard it against who?"

"Tomorrow. I'll tell you all about it tomorrow."

Gregg frowned. "Is this another one of those promises, like you made that schoolteacher?" he asked.

Flem's eyes opened wide, as if he suddenly remembered. "Oh my God!" he exclaimed. "Miss Colburn! She'll skin me alive!" He turned to Gregg. "Now listen careful, boy. I'm gonna give you your first assignment. I want you to attend the meeting of the Better Riley Committee and then first thing in the morning I want you to write a story about it. You understand? They're meeting at the school, just up—"

"I know where the school is, but don't you think I'm a little late? The meeting started at seven, more than two hours ago."

"You never can tell about those meetings. Two hours ago you say?"

"It's nine-fifteen."

"In case it's over, go to the house right behind the school building, the little house. Looks like a doll house. Belle Colburn lives there. She'll tell you everything that happened at the meeting."

"Where will you be?"

"Wes and I have some business over at the office."

"What kind of business?"

Wes grinned. "Persistent, ain't he? Natural born newsman, Flem. Goes after a story just like a hound dog, once he gets the scent."

"You're obviously expecting trouble. Why can't you tell me what it is?" asked Gregg impatiently.

"Tell ya all about it tomorrow," said Flem. "That's a promise. Right, Wes? That's a promise. Right?"

"It better be. He'll pester the daylights outa ya if it isn't. It better be a promise that's kept."

"Tomorrow, Gregg. I'll tell ya all about it. That's a promise. You'll cover the assignment I gave you, right? She's a wonderful lady, Miss Colburn, a great schoolteacher. She'll be very disappointed if we don't have a good story about that committee meeting."

Gregg nodded. "I'll take care of it."

"You should enjoy it."

Gregg nodded. "Yeah, sure." There was nothing he would enjoy more than interviewing a spinster schoolteacher on the latest happenings of the Better Riley Committee. "I can hardly wait," he said glumly.

CHAPTER 6

If Riley shattered Gregg's illusions about western towns, Belle Colburn exploded his image of western schoolteachers. She was as young and lively as a freshly washed pair of skin tight jeans. Her round face glowed, without any trace of makeup. Her brown eyes were fueled with enthusiasm.

She leaned in the doorway, her shirttail hanging loose, while Gregg introduced himself. She seemed amused when he tried to apologize for his uncle.

"I never figured he'd make it," she said. "Not after I learned Wes Darby was in town."

She had to tilt her slender head back to look up into his eyes. It gave her a tomboy look, until Gregg noticed the top button on her shirt wasn't buttoned. The swell below it caught his eye.

She looked at him with a mischievous little smile, as if she knew something he didn't and she was debating whether or not to tell him.

"I'm supposed to find out what happened at your meeting and write it up for the paper," he said.

"Oh you are." That little smile seemed to brighten. She stepped back inside. "Come in," she said.

It was a small house, divided into four equal-sized rooms; two bedrooms, a living room, and a kitchen. The wood floors were level, which was unusual for a western house. Gregg decided it was because the place was new and hadn't had time to settle. He sat on a long sofa that looked like something from an old hotel. It was covered with bright red calico, matching the red calico curtains.

"This your place?" he asked.

"It comes with the job. Actually it's your uncle's. He donated it to the school."

"I didn't know Uncle Flem was so civic-minded."

"A lot of people don't."

"Have you known him long?"

"Just since I got here, three years ago. He's like a father and a friend."

"I never met anybody that knew that side of him."

"What side of him have you heard about?"

"He's restless, moves a lot. Has a weakness for whiskey, women, and gambling."

Belle laughed. "That's Flem!" She had an infectious laugh. There was a possessive quality about the way she laughed over Flem, about the way she talked about Flem. Gregg had the feeling they were talking about her uncle instead of his.

He sat on the long couch. She sat in a rocking chair

to one side.

"Do you want to tell me about the meeting?" he asked. She paused, her eyes twinkling again. Whatever secret it was that she was thinking about sharing with him, it sure amused her.

"When did you get to town?" she asked.

"This afternoon."

"He sure didn't waste any time."

"Whata ya mean by that?"

"Sending you by."

"It's my first assignment in the newspaper business!"

"He knows I'll write an article about the meeting."

Gregg looked puzzled. "I don't understand. Why'd he send me to . . ."

"Your uncle is a manipulator."

"What's he manipulating?"

"Us. He's trying to match us."

"Oh, for gosh sakes!"

"Don't flatter yourself. Every single man in this town has been by here at some time or another on an errand for your uncle."

"He wants you married?"

"He wants me nailed down—in Riley. It's flattering, but embarrassing at times."

"You must be awful hard to please if he hasn't sent one yet that sticks."

"I don't think I'm hard to please. It's just that right now I'd rather do what I'm doing than darn socks and wash diapers."

"Independent, eh?"

"No different from a lot of other women in this part of the country."

"What do you do that you enjoy so much?"

"I have some unusually gifted students, like Dora Benson for example. They say her mother was a whore and her father a gambler. She and her mother work at a ranch home during the summer and live here the rest of the time. She's grown up with some strange ideas, particularly about men. But she's sharp as a tack and it's exciting for me, as her teacher, to see a girl like Dora come alive, to watch her mind develop. I'm hoping for her to get more schooling in San Francisco.

"And then there are the committees I work on that's literally changed the face of this town. We've got a flower garden contest going that's gotten half the families in town interested in planting flowers. We shamed the town council into building the best boardwalk on each side of Main Street that you'll find in the West. Now we're working on the merchants to keep it clean, and they're doing it. The railroad wouldn't spend a dime on the depot, until our committee sent a special delegation all the way to Cheyenne to talk to some of the directors. Now we've got the brightest, cleanest depot in the Territory.

"I enjoy getting involved in things like that. I enjoy seeing a job that needs to be done and then figuring a way to do it. I enjoy seeing the results of my work."

Gregg smiled at her enthusiasm. "You enjoy life."

"I guess that is it. I enjoy life!"

"I can see why Uncle Flem wants you to stay in Riley. You're good for the town."

She laughed. It was a rich, contagious laugh. "Flem wouldn't give two fingers of whiskey for every flower garden, boardwalk, and new coat of paint in town.

He's big on education, but all the rest is like a lace tablecloth to him. He'd just as soon eat off a log. He wants me to stay in Riley because I'm the only person in town he can discuss literature with. He once kept me up half the night talking about Dante's *Inferno*"

"And you loved it."

"And I loved it!"

A pretty young schoolteacher, full of life, and a tired old newspaperman, full of the devil. It was a combination Gregg could appreciate. He was happy for both of them.

"You must know a lot about my uncle," he said.

"Flem is a very private man. He puts most of himself in his paper. What's left gets pretty evenly divided between myself, Harry Pratt, the bartender at Ryan's Saloon, visiting newspaper editors, and a handful of friends in town."

"Just a handful?"

"Old timers mostly. You might as well learn it right off, Gregg. Your uncle isn't very popular among businessmen. They say he's out of tune with the times. To them business is everything and anybody who thinks different is the enemy."

"Does my uncle think different?"

"Frequently. The biggest example was when Felix Kassner got the town all excited over the possibility of his railroad building a rolling mill here. Kassner said he favored building it here over any other town along the line, and he was sure he could get his board of directors to agree, if the town would show enough interest. It meant two hundred seventy new jobs, which is quite a payroll for a town this size. Well, other towns wanted it too, so Kassner got them bidding against each other. First one town would offer one thing and then another would offer a little extra, then Riley offered still more. The Riley Town Council offered to cut all taxes on the new mill for ten years and to reduce the taxes Kassner Enterprises now pays on railroad property in town by thirty percent. Bensenville offered to cut all taxes on all railroad property for ten years and pledged to sell bonds for a twenty-four thousand dollar donation toward the construction of the rolling mill.

"The Town Council was about to match that offer until the *Gazette* came out with screaming editorials charging the railroad with robbing the citizens of Riley to stuff business profits into the cash boxes of merchants. Flem said nobody in their right mind wanted a rolling mill in their town anyhow, because of the noise and smoke it would produce. Needless to say, he wasn't very popular with local businessmen who wanted to cash those two hundred seventy paychecks every week."

"What happened to the rolling mill?"

"It's in Bensenville which is now a larger and wealthier town than Riley; it's also a noisier town and a smoke-stained town. Sometimes in the winter when the mill's going full blast and there's a coal fire in every building in town the air gets so full of coal soot you can't see the sun at high noon. Everybody has a black nose from breathing the stuff."

"The price of progress."

"A lot of folks are willing to pay it. But not Flem. He'll pay just so much, then he comes out kicking and screaming."

"Who is Kassner?"

"He built the railroad and owns a lot of land around here, as well as some mining properties. He's a very shrewd businessman."

"My uncle was writing an editorial about him in the saloon."

Belle frowned, a trace of fear creasing her eyes. "When?" she asked.

"Just now. They took it to the Gazette building when they left the saloon."

Her eyes opened with sudden alarm. "The Gazette building! At this time of night?"

"They said something about guarding the press."

"Oh no!"

"Do you know what they were talking about?"

"If it's what I think it is, it could be trouble—big trouble!"

There were two sudden explosions, like both barrels of a shotgun firing almost simultaneously, followed by a fast series of shots, either pistol or rifle. They came from Main Street. Belle turned white. "Oh God, no!" she screamed, running out the door.

"It could be from the saloon," said Gregg, running behind her.

People came out of homes and buildings, looking around for some signs of a shooting. If it was trouble—and that many shots usually was—nobody wanted to miss seeing it. In a very few minutes Main Street was as full as it was on a busy afternoon. Most came more or less as they were, fearing they'd miss something if they took time to dress properly. Several women had on housecoats and the men had pants hurriedly pulled over flannel pajamas. Men poured out of both saloons.

"It came from the Gazette building," some one shouted. "The sheriff's already there!"

Everybody drifted toward the Gazette building. Deputy Sheriff Floyd Hammer came out the front door, looking grim. He closed the door and stood in front of it, as if guarding it.

"Nobody's allowed inside," he said. "Sheriff's orders." Then he recognized Belle and nodded, his thin lips forming a firm straight line. "Sorry, Miss Colburn, but the sheriff said nobody." A crowd quickly gathered, buzzing with excitement.

Gregg stepped forward. "I'm Gregg Martin, Flem's nephew."

"I'll tell the sheriff you're here," said the deputy, backing into the building and closing the door behind him.

In a moment Sheriff Boyd Richie stepped out, his hat pushed back on his head. He looked tired and quietly angry. Gregg figured he was one of the old timers Belle had mentioned, people like Flem who weren't in complete tune with the times. The sheriff had a softness to his gut, but a hardness in his square jaw and steel blue eyes.

"It was a bad shooting," he said. "Flem and Wes Darby are both dead. One other man, a saddle tramp it looks like, is also dead. At least one got away. Maybe more."

Belle gasped, choking a sob. Gregg put his arm around her shoulder and squeezed gently. "Who's the saddle tramp?" he asked.

The sheriff answered slowly, weighing his words. "Don't know yet. Near as we can tell, Flem and Wes were sitting on the floor, leaning against the wall near the press. God only knows what they were doing there. Never any telling with those two. These strangers broke through the back window with dynamite. I figure they were either after Flem's press, aiming to blow it to smithereens, or else they planned to bust through the wall of the Gazette building and get to the vault in the bank next door. Can't say which they had in mind, not yet anyway.

"Flem cut loose with his shotgun and Wes with a pistol. They put enough lead in the dead man to sink a ship. The man, or men, that got away musta emptied two six shooters into Flem and Wes. They aren't a pretty sight."

"Is the coroner here yet?" asked Gregg.

"He's on his way. Hope you won't take offense, being Flem's only kin, but I don't want nobody inside until the coroner gets here."

Gregg nodded. "No offense taken. Got any plans for going after the killer, or killers?"

"I'll get a tracker first thing in the morning, see if we can pick up a trail. The odds are against it. Too many horses running around these days. But we might get lucky. I got a good tracker."

"I'll tag along if you don't mind."

"Welcome the company. We'll start early, before people start moving around, making new tracks everywhere, and covering up the ones there now."

Gregg and Belle walked silently back to her home. Inside she got a bottle and two glasses from the kitchen. "Flem always kept a bottle here," she said. "I guess it's yours now."

She poured each of them a couple of fingers. Belle got a pitcher of water and filled her glass with it.

Gregg took his straight.

"Who would want to blow up Flem's press?" he asked.

"What makes you so sure they were after his press?"

"The last thing Flem said before he and Wes left me was something about guarding his press. That's why they left the saloon and went to the Gazette office."

"Guarding it against who?"

"He didn't say."

"I've been afraid something like this would happen. A lot of people don't like Flem."

"Name a few."

"George Fletcher, a small rancher with big ideas who ran against Boyd Richie for sheriff. Flem wrote editorials that cut George Fletcher to pieces. He wanted Richie for sheriff. Mat Walters owns property down by the creek that was to have been the site for the rolling mill. Walters stood to make a nice profit off of that piece of property and he'd planned to sell more lots to mill workers for home sites. He was real bitter when the mill went to Bensenville and blamed Flem for the whole thing. There isn't a mine owner in the Territory that don't hate Flem's guts for writing about Chinese coolies as if they should be treated like ordinary people. And then there's Felix Kassner, who has a special hatred for Flem. Your uncle opposed almost everything Kassner's done in this part of the country. He thinks Kassner is arrogant and greedy and completely selfish.

"All of those men, and more, would love to silence Flem's editorial blasts."

"I'm sure Kassner wouldn't want to read the editorial Uncle Flem was preparing for him."

"Did he say why he was writing it?"

"No."

"There's been a lot of talk about establishing the Wyoming Territory and setting up a territorial government. Kassner might be planning something along those lines."

"Do you think Kassner has political ambitions?"

"You can bet he will have a say in any territorial government that's established. Kassner has business associates from coast to coast, including some prominent people in Washington. He'll have a say all right, a big say."

"That might explain the editorial. Uncle Flem don't want Kassner to have a say."

Belle nodded. As long as they talked she remained completely composed. But when the conversation drew to a close her lip began to quiver. She took deep swallows of her bourbon and water.

"You gonna be all right?" asked Gregg.

"Sure."

He emptied his drink and got up to leave. "You sure?" He put his hand on her shoulder and looked into her eyes. It was like pushing down on a pump handle. Tears gushed forward. Her soft mouth became distorted in an anguished cry. Gregg put his arms around her, feeling her entire body shake.

"He was like a father to me, Gregg, the kind of father every girl dreams of having."

"I know. I know."

She pulled back, standing straight and wiping her eyes with a sleeve. She threw her head back. "I guess you've got a busy day tomorrow."

"Yes."

"I haven't had a good cry like that in years!"

"It's good for you."

"It gets off a lot of steam."

"You had a lot to let off. In a way, you're more kin to Flem than I am."

"I feel that way, but then maybe I'm just selfish."

"You're not selfish."

"You've been a big comfort. Thank you." She sounded almost formal, standing erect and distant, as if she feared his touch. "Good night, Gregg."

He felt a slight emptiness as he nodded. "Good night." He touched the door and turned, just as her eyes again swelled with tears. He held her tight, very tight. He again felt warm tears on her cheek.

"There, there," he whispered. "I'm right here. I'll be right here as long as you need me." He kept holding her until her body stopped trembling, then picked her up and carried her to the bedroom.

She fell asleep in his arms.

The next morning Sheriff Richie, Alvaro Cortes, as the tracker, and Gregg sat in the sheriff's office with tin cups of steaming coffee, waiting for enough daylight to start looking for tracks.

Cortes, half Mexican and half Apache had left his home country in the hills of Arizona and New Mexico when it became unhealthy for breeds to live with the warring factions developing there. The whites either killed or ostracized any man with dark skin, black hair, and brown eyes. The Mexicans feared the Apache blood in Cortes and the Apaches had no respect for his reluctance to kill and plunder Mexican ranches.

Cortes became a lone hunter, surviving by tracking game in areas where many experienced hunters claimed game no longer existed. He was a bounty hunter for a short period. Tracking men was much easier than tracking game, but he quickly lost his taste for it. Cortes did not enjoy killing.

Law officers began hiring him to track down killers, bank robbers, and, in at least two instances, runaway husbands. He did not mind this kind of work. Others made the arrests or did the shooting. All Cortes did was follow the trail and show the way. He soon had a reputation as one of the best trackers in the West.

A short, intense man, Cortes talked little as they started looking at footprints and marks in the dusty alley behind the Gazette building. He kneeled, walked gingerly around a heel print, then kneeled again, studying marks in the thick dust. "Two men," he said, using a stick to outline two distinct sets of footprints going toward the building. "One man," he added, pointing to one print, less distinct, going west, away from the building. "He run," he said, pointing to the heavy print of the front of the shoe and only a slight trace of a heel print.

Cortes studied the footprints carefully, as if committing them to memory, before moving on. There was no hurrying him.

At the end of the alley, which ran parallel to Main Street, the tracks were lost in a sea of boot and hoof prints. "Everybody in town must have walked by here last night, wanting to see what the commotion was all about," said Sheriff Richie.

"If those two men walked up this alley, and one of

them ran out of the alley, where were their horses?"
asked Gregg.

"My guess is they left them outside of town," said
the sheriff. "Strangers on horseback would have been
noticed after an explosion. Men on foot could hide in
the shadows."

Gregg tried to put himself in the killer's shoes. "Is
there a spot nearby, on the edge of town, that's away
from houses, say in a clump of trees or at the base of a
hill, or—"

"In a creekbed!" said the sheriff. Cortes nodded and
they mounted up, heading southwest, toward a creek
that circled the town. As soon as they got to it the
tracker headed downstream, following the creek bank.
He signaled for the sheriff and Gregg to go upstream.
In a very few minutes the tracker emitted a shrill
whistle. The sheriff and Gregg wheeled around and
galloped downstream to join him. He was squatting
over a set of hoof prints, studying them carefully.
Footprints, made by the same two sets of boots that
had left their mark in the alley were clearly imprinted
in the soft soil. There were horse droppings and
dozens of clear hoof prints where the horses had been
tied.

The tracker, his eyes down, walked across the shallow creek, looked up and down the creekbed on the
other side, then went down a few yards before climbing up the bank. Once on flat, dry land he studied the
ground a long moment after Gregg and the sheriff
joined him. Suddenly he pointed northwest. "That
way," he said.

Gregg looked at the sheriff. "Any idea where he
headed?" The sheriff squinted at the hills immedi-

ately ahead. "Hard to say. Several ranches over that rise. Then again he might ride over that first hill, double back, and head for Bensenville, or points south."

Cortes, his eyes glued down, trotted on ahead.

The trail doubled back a couple of times, going into the creek, but each time the tracker readily picked up signs where the two horses had emerged from the creek and headed west. After doubling back twice the rider apparently figured he had eluded anybody trailing him or else he was in such a hurry he was willing to take that chance. There were no more double backs and for the rest of the morning the trail was as easy to follow as a country road.

Gregg rode close to Sheriff Richie. "Whata ya think?"

"Hard to say. There's a dozen places up ahead where he could slip out of this canyon and double back on us, head off in any direction he wants. I aim to follow the tracker, slow and sure, before I plan any moves."

"Where does this canyon lead?"

"To Severn's Valley. Good cattle country. Marble Creek goes right through it."

"Who owns it?"

"Most of it belongs to Felix Kassner. He built a big home in the hills, just across the valley, a couple a hours ride from here, only uses it summers." He chuckled. "Pretty nice I reckon, being rich."

"Our man could be headed for Kassner's."

The sheriff shrugged. "Could be headed anywhere."

"I think I'll ride on ahead. If the trail cuts back I'll see ya in town. If he heads off in another direction leave word with any ranch hand you run across. I'll follow you."

Sheriff Richie frowned. "The tracker is slow, Gregg. But he's sure. I hope you don't go off half-cocked."

"If he's gone to Kassner's place I wanta try to get there before he leaves."

"Ain't likely he'd hang around there long, even if that's where he's headed."

"Maybe not, but—"

The sheriff looked at Gregg sternly. "You know something about Kassner you ain't telling me?"

"Just that he and my uncle didn't exactly hit it off."

"That's a fact. But then your uncle didn't hit it off with a lot of men."

The tracker didn't even look up when Gregg galloped by. Cortes walked his horse slowly, his eyes darting restlessly from a scratch on a rock to a broken twig to a pair of hoof prints in sandy soil.

It was slow, tedious work, tracking.

CHAPTER 7

When Jamie McPherson brought the news of the killings Felix Kassner became hysterical. In the six years Bert Tyson had worked for him, he'd never seen Kassner go so completely loco.

The two men were behind closed doors in Kassner's study. Kassner paced back and forth behind his massive desk, his eyes as wild as a fox in a forest fire. "I didn't say to kill anybody!" he screamed. "You've ruined me!"

"Weren't supposed to be no killings," replied Bert, trying to remain calm. He crossed his legs in the straight-backed chair, trying to make himself comfortable.

"I'm ruined! Ruined!" Kassner's eyes blazed with panic as he paced back and forth. "People in Washington will connect me with those killings. The President will never appoint me!"

"Now hold on a minute," said Tyson patiently. "How can anybody connect you?"

"It's common knowledge that I hate Flem Martin."

"So do a lot of other people."

"Wes Darby probably blabbed about my trying to buy the *Gazette.*"

"I doubt it. Wes Darby ain't the kind to talk about his business with anybody. But even if he did, what's wrong with your trying to buy a newspaper? You're a businessman."

"One of the men who did it is still loose. If they catch him and. . . ."

"Danny did time in Yuma prison. He ain't about to get caught again. He'll shoot it out first."

"They'll have that Indian fellow, that tracker, after him. If they catch him, he'll talk. They'll make him talk!"

"There's only one name he could give, and that would be mine." Tyson paused, his eyes hardening. "I've been dealing with men like Danny for a long time, Mr. Kassner. There's one thing all of them know about me, and they know it well. If they squeal on me, there's an instant price on their head and a big one. I knew a deputy sheriff once that arrested a man who'd just done a job for me, a man named Jake Palmer. The deputy trailed Jake all the way to New Mexico. Jumped him one night on the desert. Jake offered that deputy a deal. He said he'd testify in court that I'd hired him for the job, if there wouldn't be no charges filed against him. Poor dumb Jake. That deputy shot him on the spot, took his gun belt, and left his carcass for the buzzards. Just as soon as that deputy told me what he'd done and showed me the gun belt as proof, I paid him off—three thousand dollars, cash money. I know, that's a lot of money. But it's worth it to me for men to know that death is as certain as a sunset if they double-cross me."

Kassner wasn't even listening. His panic-stricken thoughts were on the one fear that bothered him most. "There'll be rumors—in Washington," he said, his head falling forward. His voice was almost a sob. "A thing like this can alter history," he said. Then he looked up, his eyes growing wide. "A rumor is all it will take, a mere hint of impropriety and President Grant will refuse my appointment. Do you know what that appointment means to me, Mr. Tyson? It means the Kassner name will have a title, a title! It means I can return to Europe as a head of state! It means the board of directors of Kassner Enterprises will become my advisors, my subjects—not my equals. Their vote will have only as much power as I want to grant!"

His eyes were flashing now. His mouth spewed saliva as his voice became louder and more shrill.

My God, thought Tyson. *He has no idea how government works in the United States. He must think he's still in Austria, that he is being considered for some kind of royal post. The man is mad!*

"All of this is mine if nobody connects me with those killings!" raved Kassner.

Tyson nodded. "I'll do what I can, Mr. Kassner." He wasn't sure he was even heard.

Jamie McPherson was waiting when Tyson came out of the house. "I didn't ride all the way out here just to tell you about the killings," he said. "We got a bigger problem than that, named Case Anders."

"Who the hell is Case Anders?"

"A tinhorn gambler that Gregg Martin picked up in the hills, half bullwhipped to death. LaVida took 'em in to mend."

"She's put Case in the main house and has taken personal charge. She's with him constantly!"

"So what? She does the same thing with sick cats and sick cows."

"But this is different, Bert. She's a different person since he came. It's like there's something inside her that glows, the—" Jamie paused, looking down. "She's moonstruck, Bert. That's the plain truth of the matter. She's as moonstruck as some kid at his first barn dance."

Bert couldn't imagine it. LaVida, his loyal, long-suffering wife—moonstruck over a gambler? He would have laughed if Jamie hadn't been so dead serious.

"I know there's no love lost between you two," said Jamie. "Everybody knows you spend more time with Shelly than you do with her. She knows it too. But from a practical standpoint you better remember that you married a piece of land as well as a woman. If LaVida splits with that tinhorn, she might just get herself a sharp lawyer and take half our ranch with her—the best half."

"So it's your job you're worried about?"

"You bet your sweet ass!"

"Go on back and keep an eye on 'em. I'll be in touch."

LaVida run off with a gambler? Preposterous! She would never dream of such a thing. Still, stranger things had happened. Who would have dreamed Shelly would start acting like she was acting lately?

Bert felt like taking a long ride alone. He always felt like that when he had some thinking to do. He saddled a quarter horse and headed for the ridge trail. For a half hour he climbed, ducking branches and weaving in the saddle when the horse cut expertly back and forth scampering up the hill. Just getting up to the crest of the ridge occupied his full attention, but once there the trail leveled off and the going was easy. His thoughts drifted quickly to his problems.

Kassner was bad enough, worrying himself to death about that fool appointment. But Kassner wasn't as big a problem as the women in his life. Bert Tyson had always had a woman in his life, most of the time two or three, and the thought of living without any was like not living at all.

There was Shelly, talking again about splitting. Just last night she'd refused to come to his cabin and she didn't backslide when he pressured her either. Now LaVida was making noises that made Jamie think she was about to split too. If that was true, he was really in trouble.

Jamie was wrong when he said there was no love between him and LaVida. LaVida was raised to believe that a woman married once and stayed married no matter what. She was taught that a wife managed a household, raised kids if there were any to raise, and spread her legs when her husband told her, whether there was any feeling on her part or not. That's the way she'd been raised and that's the way she was. Bert Tyson liked having a woman like that for a wife.

The only thing bad about it was it got confining at

times. That's why Bert needed somebody like Shelly to run to on occasion, somebody he could see when he wanted and leave when he wanted. Shelly had a lot of experience with men that LaVida didn't have. She knew things that pleased a man. But Shelly could never replace LaVida, never. Shelly was a whore. In Bert's eyes, she'd always be a whore.

A man needed a whore, and a man needed a wife. A man needed both.

Bert wondered if Jamie hadn't gotten spooked over nothing. He was awful young and went off half-cocked sometimes. LaVida just wasn't the kind of woman to take up with another man, not as long as she was married. It just wasn't like her at all.

Still, he guessed he'd better go on back to the ranch and make sure the fences were mended. No sense taking chances he didn't have to take. Just as soon as he got things straightened out with Shelly, he'd go back.

Actually, he didn't have a problem with Shelly. His problem was with Dora. She'd been bad enough before she got the drop on Danny. Since then she was impossible. She was the one who put Shelly up to not coming to his cabin last night. It was all Dora's fault!

If Danny had just put the bit in her mouth instead of letting himself get caught off guard, things would be different. He would have taught her what everybody has to learn at some time or another—that nothing in life comes free. Everybody has to pay somebody.

Once Dora learned that she would look at things different. She would know that if it wasn't for Bert her mother would be back on the line, humping for enough to eat and a place for the two of them to sleep. The price Bert asked was little enough for what he'd done for them. Hell, if it wasn't for Bert, Shelly would have nothing to look forward to but spending her old age in some cowboy's lean-to, cooking over an open fire, and getting humped in a bed of half straw and half manure.

Shelly should have taught Dora those things instead of letting that schoolteacher fill the girl's head with a lot of crazy ideas. Shelly should have taught her daughter that there's a price tag on life, and she was going to have to pay it just like everybody else. But instead of teaching her, Shelly let Dora cloud her thinking with a lot of crazy ideas about freedom. Damn!

The more Bert thought about Dora the more convinced he became that she was the root of all his problems. If he could just figure some way to get rid of her, everything else would fall into place.

That teacher had talked about getting Dora enrolled in some school in San Francisco. It had seemed like a harebrained scheme to Bert, sending a girl all the way to San Francisco for schooling. A boy might go to learn the law or doctoring or something useful. But what was the use of sending a girl? What the hell good would it do her? All of a sudden it didn't seem like such a harebrained scheme to Bert. Not any more. He might just look up that teacher next time he was in town. He might even put a little money in the kitty to send Dora away.

He hadn't been paying any attention to where he was going, just sitting and letting the horse set his own pace. He wasn't even sure where he was when he first saw movement in the canyon below. It was some distance off. He wasn't sure at first it wasn't a tumbleweed riding a wind. He stopped and took a careful look. It wasn't a tumbleweed.

A lone rider was coming slowly toward him leading a second horse. Bert watched until he recognized Danny, then he wheeled his horse around, walked gingerly down the side of the hill opposite the canyon until he was out of sight. He raced across the side of the hill until he got to the neck of the canyon. He dismounted, tied his horse to a bush, pulled out his rifle and walked over the crest of the ridge, watching Danny closely as he came nearer. He kicked stones and scrub growth from behind a waist-high boulder, making a place to sit and hide. Then he sat, and waited.

He could hear the two horses breathing deep and snorting when he leaned the rifle across the boulder, getting a bead on Danny's head.

"You're headed the wrong way, Danny," he said calmly.

Danny was so startled he almost jumped out of the saddle. When he recognized Bert he smiled. "You done caused a brown spot on the seat of my pants, Bert!"

"You might just get a hole clean through those pants if you ain't careful, Danny. Yer supposed to be headed for Texas."

"Jim got it."

"I heard."

"It was Jim that wanted to go to Texas. I ain't left nothing there."

"You ain't left nothing here either."

"I figure I have."

"This rifle here says you haven't. If Kassner knew I

was even talking with ya he'd kill the both of us."

"What the hell for? I took care a Flem Martin. He'll never cause no more problems for nobody."

"Kassner figures somebody might connect the killing to him. He'd be certain of it if he knew you were anywhere in these parts."

"Now just how in the hell are they gonna connect me with him? I've never even seen the man!"

"Who knows what you'd say, Danny—if they pressed you hard enough."

"I know better than to cross you, Bert. I don't claim to be bright, but I know that much."

Bert nodded. "Kassner isn't so sure of that, Danny. He'd order you killed in a minute if he knew you were on his land."

"It would be a lot simpler if somebody just left a fresh horse and some supplies near the corral. I'd be heading south in no time—out of everybody's hair."

"Texas?"

"Maybe even Mexico. All it takes is a horse, some grub, and—and her."

"Don't tell me you've still got a hard on for Dora?"

"That's why I came back, Bert. She's the only reason I came back. I don't plan to leave without her either."

"You're thinking with your cock!"

"I'm thinking it's to your advantage to help me, Bert. Did I tell you what she said when she backed me out the door with my gun? She said you would get the same, only worse, one of these days if you didn't leave her mom alone. That's what she said, Bert."

"She's just a child, filled with a lot of crazy ideas."

"She's a woman now, Bert, tough as baked leather."

"I've a mind to pull this trigger, Danny, and just leave your carcass for the buzzards."

"A lot of folks might wonder why I came here, Bert."

Bert smiled. "Who'd know? You wouldn't be the first stranger to these parts who drifted in but never drifted out and nobody knowed what happened."

"I hear the sheriff has a topnotch tracker working for him these days. Part Apache they say." He grinned confidently. "I left a trail a blind man could follow, Bert. Oh, I doubled back a couple of times, to slow 'em down some. But I suspect they'll be along, sooner or later."

"Ride ahead," said Bert, motioning with his rifle. "I'll think on it as we ride in."

"If they track me to the ranch and find I've left these two old nags and stole a fresh horse and picked me up a hostage to boot, they may not even suspect that we know one another."

"They'd track ya down, Danny."

Danny's face became deadly serious. "No man can track me across rock and shale."

Gregg rode out of the canyon into Severn's Valley, then across the valley to Marble Creek where he watered Skala and stretched his legs. He followed the creek until he came to a wide, flat spot where somebody had recently camped. Tins and bottles littered the area. There were old hoof prints, identical to ones they had been following.

He found a trail leading into the hills behind the creek, in the direction Sheriff Richie had said Kassner's ranch was located. He took it and in less than an hour saw the corral and stables, and then the clump of cabins surrounding Kassner's large home.

He had obviously followed a trail through wooded hill country that brought him in the back way to the ranch. As he crossed the cleared land, heading toward the corral and stables he looked around nervously. It could be dangerous if he was mistaken for a trespasser.

"That's far enough, mister!" came a shout from inside the stables.

Gregg stopped and looked vainly for a face to go with the deep, harsh voice. "Climb down and reach!"

Gregg stepped down, standing to one side of his horse, and raised his hands.

Bert Tyson stepped out of the stable, his rifle aimed at Gregg's gut. "What's yer business?"

"Name's Gregg Martin. Flem Martin's my uncle."

"What brings you here?"

"I want to see Felix Kassner."

"What about?"

"Are you Kassner?"

"No, but this rifle says you better answer my question."

"Kassner might not like another Martin getting gunned down, this time right under his nose."

"Walk in front of me, smart ass. If you even act like you're reaching for iron you'll be doing me a favor."

They walked up a grassy knoll past the cabins to the main house. Shelly was watching them from the back door.

"Tell Mr. Kassner he's got a visitor," said Tyson. "Claims to be Flem Martin's nephew."

Shelly disappeared and in a few minutes returned.

"He says to come in." She looked at Tyson. "He says for you to come in with him."

"You heard her, smart ass," said Tyson, poking Gregg painfully in the back with the barrel of his rifle.

Gregg appeared to stumble as he stepped inside the door, bending to catch his balance. Suddenly he twirled around, his left arm lashing against the barrel of Tyson's rifle, knocking it to one side. With his right hand Gregg drew his pistol and rammed it deep into Tyson's gut. "Now you lead the way, smart ass," he said, taking the rifle.

Tyson walked ahead, rubbing the soreness in his belly where the pistol barrel had sunk deep. He walked through the kitchen and down a hall to a dark, heavy door. He knocked lightly.

"Come," commanded Felix Kassner.

Bert opened the door and led the way into the study. Kassner was sitting at his huge desk in the middle of the room, looking like a midget in the chair of a giant. Shelves of papers and books covered the wall on each side of him. Behind him was a large window, allowing light to flow over his shoulders. More light came from a skylight immediately over his head. Kassner nodded to two straightbacked chairs in front of his desk. Tyson and Gregg sat down, uncomfortably. Kassner preferred guests in his study to be uncomfortable. That way they wouldn't take so much of his time.

"I was sorry to hear about your uncle," he said mechanically. "Hopefully we will civilize this country soon and these acts of violence will cease."

"I was under the impression you two didn't see eye to eye on many things," said Gregg.

"Your uncle didn't see eye to eye with a lot of people,

people who want to see this territory prosper and progress. But that doesn't excuse violence."

"He liked the old ways."

Tyson was relieved to see Kassner his old self, collected and calm.

Kassner smiled. "I often had the impression he would prefer the ways of the Indians," he said.

"His killer headed toward your ranch, Mr. Kassner."

The bluntness of that piece of information startled Kassner, visibly. Tyson wondered if Gregg Martin hadn't planned it that way, hoping to throw him off balance.

"How do you know that?" asked Kassner, recovering his composure quickly.

"I just left Sheriff Richie and a tracker about two hours ago. They're heading this way. Should be halfway across Severn's Valley by now."

"You are assuming of course that the killer went across Severn's Valley."

"He camped on Marble Creek, for several days if the garbage pile is any indication. I figure they camped there until they decided to blow up the *Gazette*, or until they got orders to do it."

"What makes you so certain they intended to blow up the *Gazette*, Mr. Martin. I understand some people think they intended to gain access to the bank through a common wall separating the bank from the Gazette building."

"I don't happen to believe that."

"Really."

"I happen to believe they were paid to blow up the *Gazette's* press and that my uncle and Wes Darby knew they were coming and that's why they were guarding it."

"What makes you think they were guarding your uncle's press?"

"Because they told me!"

"Who else did they tell this?"

"Nobody! There was just the three of us."

Kassner nodded, smiling. "I see."

"What do you see, Mr. Kassner?"

"Your motive for coming here, of course. It is blackmail, is it not?"

"What the hell are you talking about?"

"Come, come, Mr. Martin. I understand these things. How much? How much do you want to not spread the ridiculous rumor that the killer came here and that the victims were guarding the press as you put it, rumors that you know you could never prove, but some people would believe anyhow. I abhor blackmail, but I'm a reasonable man. If you have a reasonable figure in mind, I might be persuaded to—"

"I'm beginning to see why my uncle hated your guts."

Gregg walked to the door, slamming it shut as he left. He nodded at a silent, frightened-looking Shelly as he went through the kitchen and out the back door. He hadn't gone ten yards when Bert caught up with him. It was a very different Bert Tyson from the man who'd held him at the end of a carbine only a few minutes earlier.

"Now hold up a second, young fella," said Bert, smiling. Gregg couldn't believe it at first. "We got off on the wrong foot, but that's no reason to—"

"Why'd you pull a rifle on me?"

"How'd I know you was who you said you was?"

"How do you now?"

"It's obvious now. I don't want no hard feelings, not with Flem Martin's nephew. Can't we patch this up?"

Shelly came out the door and walked past them without saying a word. She disappeared in the farthest cabin.

"How can you work for a man like that?" asked Gregg.

"He pays well."

"He bribes well too."

"Mr. Kassner figures money will buy anything. Most a the time he's right."

"Not this time."

"Not with Flem either. I warned him about trying to buy Flem off. Mr. Kassner don't understand men like yer uncle and Wes Darby and—" Bert paused, smiling at Gregg. "What's next?"

"I haven't decided yet." He frowned at Bert, unable to understand why he was suddenly so friendly. "But whatever it is won't be any of your business—or his!" He motioned toward Kassner's study.

Bert's smile faded. "All right, we won't be friends," he said. "But let me tell you something that might help both of us. Mr. Kassner is a very powerful man in these parts, very powerful. He could do a lot for a young man like you. He could also do a lot to hurt a young man like you. You better think it over."

Gregg's eyes narrowed to a mere slit. "I already have," he replied slowly, accenting each word.

Shelly came running out of her cabin, her eyes wild with fear. "Bert! She's gone!" She screamed, then burst into tears. "Dora's gone!"

"What the hell are you talking about?"

"She went to the cabin, over an hour ago. She had a pair of jeans and two shirts drying on the line this morning. They're gone! Her saddle's gone!"

· "How long ago?" asked Gregg.

"An hour. Maybe an hour and a half."

"She didn't leave the back way, or I'd have seen her."

Gregg watched Bert Tyson, who didn't seem as surprised as Gregg thought he should be. He didn't seem surprised at all.

"Settle down, Shelly," said Bert. He sounded annoyed that she had interrupted them. "Dora's probably taking a ride somewhere."

"She wouldn't go for a ride without telling me!" replied Shelly.

"I'll check the road to town," said Gregg. Then he looked at Bert and moved his hand close to his holster. "And I'll have my eye on you until I'm clear a this place."

"You got me all wrong, son."

"Maybe. But don't follow me after I leave. If I draw on you again I draw firing."

Gregg backed toward the corral, boarded Skala and headed for the road leading to town.

He'd gone about a mile when he noticed fresh hoof prints to one side of the road. About a hundred yards farther he noticed them again, and then again. It looked like a high spirited horse had pranced off the road for a short distance and then been pulled back, and then it pranced off again. He wouldn't have noticed if the prints hadn't been so regular, about every hundred yards. Somebody was playing a game of some kind, riding off the road every hundred yards, for just a little piece, then getting back on. Or else they were trying to get attention. He began looking for the tracks.

He came to a long stretch of rock where even the tracker would have had trouble finding tracks. He saw nothing. But as soon as he was on sandy soil again the tracks went off the road, then came back on, then a hundred yards or so farther down they went off again. Then there was more rock and shale for a mile or more and Gregg could find no trace of anybody. As soon as there was loose dirt or sandy soil the tracks went off the road again.

The next stretch of shale ran for a couple of miles. About halfway, Gregg saw something red a good thirty yards off the roadway. It was a cotton shirt, freshly washed. It looked like a girl's shirt. It could have been a signal of some kind, but for whom? And from whom? Then again, somebody might have just lost a shirt. Gregg went back to the road and continued on. When he got out of the shale he looked for tracks off the road. There were none. He went several hundred yards farther, looking carefully, finding nothing. Suddenly he wheeled around and rode back to the spot where the shirt had been dropped. He picked it up and rode across the shale away from the road, his eyes searching for signs of tracks.

It was that missing girl, Dora. It had to be. The tracks were fresh and who else would have had a freshly laundered shirt to drop? And the person with her, forcing her to travel, had to be his uncle's killer. It was all very clear to Gregg now. The camp site below the ranch, on Marble Creek, the telltale signs of men having camped for several days—long enough for the killer to have met Dora.

The killer also knew Bert Tyson. He had to. He would never have taken a chance on coming to the ranch if he didn't know he had a friend, maybe even an accomplice, in Bert Tyson.

As soon as Gregg cleared the shale he rode back and forth along the edge until he found fresh tracks in sandy soil. There were three sets of tracks, two riders and a pack animal, he decided. The killer knew Tyson all right. He'd gotten fresh horses and supplies from Tyson. He'd also gotten himself a young traveling companion.

Gregg rode until nearly dark, then dismounted and walked his horse, easily following the well-marked trail. He stopped when he saw the tracks leading toward a butte ahead. He tied Skala near a patch of good grazing, then sat and waited until it was dark.

The moon came out bright, near full, with a clear sky. Gregg bent low, crawling at times, as he circled the butte. On the back side the rock was steep. In a wide crevice he found what he'd expected—two horses and a mule tied down for the night. The killer had made camp on top of the butte, high ground for safety and to give him a clear sight of anybody that might be following.

Gregg went a quarter of the way farther around the butte, then headed up the steep side. Halfway up he heard voices.

"The quicker you get off yer high horse, the quicker those ropes come off," came a man's voice.

If the girl responded Gregg couldn't hear her. He

edged slowly up, being careful with his footing.

The man's voice sounded again. "You aim to be like this all the way to Texas?"

"I don't aim to go to Texas," replied a female voice. Gregg was surprised at her tone, full of confidence, almost completely free of fear.

"You're going to Texas all right. You better just get used to that idea. You're going to Texas if I have to keep you hog-tied and gagged all the way."

"Then you're just gonna have to keep me hog-tied and gagged!"

The man laughed, also confidently. "Stand up," he said. "Let's see what ya look like in the moonlight."

There was a brief silence, then a loud smack of a hand on flesh.

"I said stand up!" repeated the man. There was a scuffle, a rip of clothing, heavy breathing, then the rustle of cloth. "There by God! That's better!" said the man. There was a long pause. "That's damn nice," he added.

Gregg held his breath and edged faster up the incline. His foot hit a rock which gave way, bouncing noisily down the side of the butte. Gregg stopped. He remained perfectly still, holding his breath, holding his body flat against the rocky incline. He could only hold on with his right hand, his gun hand. He reached around his side with his left, reaching toward his holster. He looked up just as his fingers touched the grip of his pistol.

He was staring straight into a pair of gleaming eyes, dark eyes. Gregg could only see the man's eyes. The rest of his face was hidden by the barrel of a pistol aimed right at Gregg's head. The barrel was so close to Gregg's face that it looked like the barrel of a cannon. "That's as far as you're going," snarled Danny.

Gregg froze, and waited.

It would come. It always came. A mistake. All men made mistakes. He concentrated on staying alert and fighting fear. His left hand had a firm grip on his pistol. He didn't move, or breathe. He just waited, and watched.

Danny's eyes glistened with confidence, the confidence of the victor. "So long, *hombre*," he said, aiming his pistol at a spot exactly between Gregg's eyes, and pulling back the hammer.

The tendency to panic was overpowering. Gregg felt his entire body start to shake. It must have had an impact on Danny, who paused to grin down at his helpless victim. "You look real pitiful, you know that?" he said.

"Who is it?" asked Dora.

Danny, supremely confident, turned to look at her. "Who was he, you mean?" he said. He savored the thrill of seeing fear now in her eyes. It made him feel powerful, a big man. He paused, basking in his new found glory with an enemy lying helpless below him and a beautiful woman shivering before his gaze. It was a moment to cherish, to relish, to stretch out.

There, thought Gregg. There is the mistake.

As Danny turned to look at Dora, his arm moved slightly to the right. The barrel of the pistol was aimed just outside of Gregg's ear. It would be corrected in a second, in a fraction of a second probably. But that's all the time Gregg needed to draw his weapon with his left hand, lift it, and fire. There was a return fire, almost a simultaneous shot, that sent a slug burning the edge of Gregg's ear. There were no more shots.

Danny's face exploded as blood, bone, and flesh erupted in all directions. His head whipped back from the impact of the bullet. He fell flat on his back, and did not move.

Gregg crawled the rest of the way up the butte and smiled at Dora. "Good timing," he said.

"Good shooting," she replied, returning his smile. "I just prayed you'd see your chance."

"I just prayed I'd get a chance."

The first thing that impressed Gregg about Dora was her complete lack of fear. She stood erect, even proud, in spite of the ropes that held her arms and legs together. Her eyes were undaunted, fiercely determined.

The second impression he had was her complete indifference to standing before him totally naked.

As she dressed, Gregg dragged Danny's body to the edge of the butte and pushed it over.

"May the varmints have a feast on his carcass," said Dora, without pity.

The next morning, over coffee, Gregg was again impressed by Dora's lack of fear. She wanted to get back to the ranch early, because she didn't want her mother worrying. But she had no fear at all of riding back alone. It was easy to see why Belle Colburn had taken a special interest in her. Dora reminded him a lot of Belle in that she was not only bright and independent, but she had a mind of her own.

He knew she and her mother worked for Kassner and probably for Bert Tyson, but he was convinced he could trust her. He had no choice but to try.

"There's a connection between Danny and Tyson and Kassner," he said. "There's bound to be."

"You'll have a hard time proving it," replied Dora. "Tyson does a good job of covering their tracks."

"Where did he get Danny?"

Dora shrugged. "The word goes out that Tyson needs men. Men drift in, hang around awhile, then drift out. Hired hands. They're all just hired hands. Danny was just a hired hand, like dozens of others Tyson's picked up. Bert Tyson used to do Kassner's dirty work himself. But here lately he's taken to hiring gunmen, drifters, cowpunchers down on their luck—anybody he can find that's handy with a gun or a stick of dynamite." She chuckled. "He's learned a lesson from Mr. Kassner I reckon—no sense sticking his neck out when he can hire it done."

"And Danny's partner, the one my uncle killed—he was just a hired hand too?"

Dora nodded. "They all are. They get paid to do a job and then skedaddle."

Gregg rubbed his chin. It wasn't going to be easy getting the men responsible for his uncle's death. Kassner was like a general, with Bert Tyson as his adjutant. Those kind never got close to the front lines, where the action was.

"There's gotta be a way to smoke them out," he said.

CHAPTER 8

Bert Tyson rode hard, as if it was his horse's fault that he felt such a painful knot in his gut—as if speed would ease the pain of it. Just who in the hell did Shelly think she was, leaving the ranch like that without a word to anybody? What the hell was she up to? Well, whatever it was, he'd soon let her know how the cow ate the cabbage. No two-bit whore was gonna treat him like this and get away with it!

He turned north before entering town, not wanting to be seen just yet. He made a wide circle and came on to the house where Shelly and Dora spent their winters from the back side.

There were four small houses in a cluster, right at the north edge of Riley. They'd all been built three years ago by a cowboy turned carpenter who lived in one, moved his elderly mother into another, and sold the other two—one to Bert Tyson and the other one to Harry Pratt. The houses were small and not very well built. Shelly and Dora almost froze that first winter, the cracks in the walls and floors were so big. They probably would have if Harry Pratt hadn't helped them chink it before the winter really socked in. Harry had also added extra support for the floor, so it didn't sag so much. The cowboy who built it wasn't much of a stickler for details.

Bert hadn't planned to buy a mansion. All he wanted was a place to keep Shelly in that was convenient for him to visit when he wanted—and that didn't cost too much.

Bert knew folks in town gossiped a lot about what a rotten thing it was for him, with a faithful wife, to buy a house to share with a whore, or rather a former whore. But he didn't give a damn what folks said. He aimed to live like he wanted to live and anybody who didn't like it could look the other way.

There was a small stable behind the house where Bert left his horse. He walked to the back door, then stopped when he heard voices from around front— voices and laughter. He heard Shelly say: "Oh, Harry! It's beautiful!" Then she laughed. Bert hadn't heard her laugh like that since he first met her, when they had fun times together. It had a sort of musical sound to it, like it came from a glow deep inside her.

Bert walked around the house and saw Shelly and Harry Pratt fiddling with a newly painted box of some kind. They were nailing it to the front of the house. They didn't see Bert at first. They were too busy looking at each other and laughing and holding the box like it might break. Shelly's eyes were bright, brighter'n Bert had ever seen them.

Harry Pratt was a runt of a man, pale from spending so much time behind a bar, with a little potbelly from joining his customers when somebody bought a round for the house. He hardly came to Bert's chin. His face was squeezed up, reminding Bert of a little puppy.

"What the hell are you two doing?" asked Bert.

Both of them jumped at the sound of his voice. "Oh, hello, Bert," said Harry. He looked like a child caught with his hand in the cookie jar.

"Harry made me a flower box," explained Shelly.

"A what?"

"A flower box. A lot of folks are building them now. We'll fill it with rich dirt and plant flowers in it."

"Oh."

"We're just about finished," said Harry, nailing a brace from a plank shelf along the window sill to the side of the house. The flower box was to sit on the shelf. Bert watched a moment, "Hurry that up, will you, Harry. I gotta talk to Shelly." He went inside and waited.

Harry finished and left for the saloon. Once again, he was late opening up. Shelly went inside to join Bert.

"Well?" he shouted.

"Well what?"

"What the hell you mean, leaving the ranch without so much as a word?"

"Mr. Kassner said it was all right."

"You could have told me you were leaving!"

"You would have just made another scene."

They were in the small kitchen. Shelly was standing by the wood stove, looking at the coffee pot. Bert reached for her, but she turned away. "Want some coffee?" she asked.

"You know what I want. Where's Dora?"

"Visiting Belle Colburn."

"Getting her head filled with ideas about going to San Francisco?"

"She's returning some books Belle loaned her."

"And borrowing more, I'll bet."

Shelly's eyes glared at him. "I hope so!"

"When are you coming back to the ranch?"

"In a few days."

Bert reached again for her arm, grabbing her this time and twirling her to face him. "What is this, Shelly?"

"I'm not going to be your woman no more, Bert. I want out."

"We've gone over that."

"I know, and I've always given in, but no more."

"How will you live?"

"We'll manage, Dora and I. We'll manage, somehow."

"How about her plans to get more schooling in San Francisco?"

"We'll work something out."

"I'll help, financially I mean. I'll help her get to San Francisco."

"You've always laughed at the idea."

"I've changed my thinking on it. I want to help."

"You just want her out of town!"

"Don't talk that way, Shelly."

"It's true isn't it? Dora's made me see what a mess

I'm making of my life, when there's no need—not any more, not now. She's made me see that I can change my life."

He let go of her arm. "I offer you a helping hand and you bite it. You bite it!"

"It won't work, Bert, not any more. The threats won't work. The offer of more help won't work. Nothing will work. I want out, and I'm going to get out!"

He backed toward the kitchen door. He'd seen her upset before, but never like this. He'd give her some time alone, to think things through. In time she'd change her mind. She always had. In time she'd see that she couldn't make it without him.

"Have a good rest," he said. "Come back to the ranch when you're ready. We'll talk then."

Shelly's eyes looked a lot like Dora's when she glared at him. They had the same fire, the same fierce determination. It made him uneasy. He left through the back door, climbed on his horse, and headed toward his ranch. He'd never seen her look that determined before.

The knot returned to his stomach, worse than before. He couldn't believe that a whore was doing this to him. It just couldn't be. Still, the knot was there, big and painful, as if he'd just lost something that meant more to him than he'd ever imagined. He had to have a drink. He had to have a drink bad.

He went to Ryan's Saloon and ordered a glass of whiskey. After he downed it hurriedly he ordered another. "Hey," he said. "Where's Harry Pratt?"

"Harry had some business at home," said the strange bartender. "He asked me to fill in for him for an hour or so." Bert chuckled cynically. "Probably making another flower box," he said. Bert was suspicious by nature, but he couldn't believe Shelly could see anything in that pale-faced, potbellied little bartender other than a friendly face to borrow a cup of sugar from, and maybe exchange flower seed with.

Bert finished his second drink, then bought a bottle and headed for his ranch. Every mile or so he'd reach in his saddlebag and pull out the bottle. By the time he got to the ranch it was half empty. Flower boxes, he thought. What the hell was the country coming to?

Jamie McPherson and Lew Rollins came out of the bunkhouse to meet him. Lew took his horse, but not before Bert took the bottle out of the saddlebag. He and Jamie walked toward the house.

"You come through Riley?" asked Jamie.

"Yep."

"Then I reckon you heard."

"Heard what?"

"About all the flowers."

Bert stopped and looked at his foreman. "What the blazes you talking about?"

Jamie stared over his shoulder, toward the veranda. "There they are," he said.

The entire veranda was covered with flower pots and boxes filled with blooming flowers. Other flowers were cut and tied in bunches.

"It's that tinhorn," explained Jamie. "He had 'em hauled out here for LaVida."

Bert walked to the veranda, growing more fierce by the second. He paused, looking at row after row of colorful pots, freshly painted boxes and brilliant flowers. He staggered to the wood pile at the side of the house, returning with an ax. He looked possessed, his face a grotesque mask of savage hate, his eyes burning with fury. He started swinging, sending sounds of destruction echoing through the stillness.

Long after the last pot was smashed, the last box was in splinters, the last flower petal scattered in dirt, he continued to swing and smash and chop. It was as if his whole world was crumbling and the flowers were to blame.

The solid and powerful Kassner was turning to quicksand. Shelly was turning her back to him, after all he'd done for her. And now LaVida, his once loyal and faithful wife, was—

He smashed the ax into a mound of dirt. "I'll kill that tinhorn bastard!" he screamed. "I'll kill him!!"

Jamie stood quietly in the shadows, a satisfied smile gleaming in his eyes. He'd always wanted to be in on a justified killing, and this one would be justified if there ever was one.

CHAPTER 9

They were in the sheriff's office, kicking the facts around again. Gregg figured if he kicked them enough, something might surface.

As far as Sheriff Richie was concerned the case was closed. The killer left a clear trail right to Kassner's ranch where he stole fresh horses, kidnapped a young girl, and headed out. The sheriff didn't say so, but he considered it fool luck that Gregg happened on his trail like he did and got the draw on him on top of that butte. Things happened that way some times. Just fool luck.

"We know two men broke into the Gazette building that night," he said. "Your uncle killed one on the spot. You killed the other." The sheriff shrugged. "That's all there is to it." The sheriff had been reading an eastern paper and still wore his glasses.

Gregg smashed his right fist into the palm of his left hand. "Damn it, sheriff! You know who's behind it all as well as I do!"

"Sure I do, but the only way the law can move on Tyson or Kassner is for somebody to testify against them. The only ones who could do that are dead." The sheriff paused, then looked at Gregg over the rims of his glasses. "We're just gonna have to be patient, young fella," he said. "They'll make a mistake one of these days. Those kind always do."

"Seems to me I've heard that before."

The sheriff smiled. "It ain't exactly an original idea."

Gregg nodded.

"I read where Congress is about to make us a bona fide territory," said the sheriff, wanting a change of topics.

"That's what I hear. Where'd they get that name Wyoming?"

"Some Congressman from Ohio suggested it. I hear he got it from some place in Pennsylvania."

"Looks like they'd check with folks who live here before they named it," said Gregg.

"Politicians don't work that way."

"They'll name a territorial governor next. Probably won't check with folks here about that either."

"Heard Kassner's name bandied about. Folks say he dearly wants the job," the sheriff said.

"Why?"

"Power, prestige, more money."

Gregg rubbed his jaw, thinking of the editorial his uncle and Wes were writing that last night. He wondered if his uncle had planned to publish it to head off Kassner being named territorial governor. Sheriff Richie looked at him as if reading his thoughts.

"You plan to put out a newspaper?" asked the Sheriff.

"Haven't decided yet. The men in the shop are busy with printing orders right now. They haven't time to print a newspaper, even if we wanted to."

"Flem never had time either. He put off the printing jobs to put out his paper."

"More money in printing."

"No fun though. Least that's what Flem used to say." The sheriff leaned forward and rummaged through some papers on his desk, picking up one and handing it to Gregg. "That was laying between yer uncle and Wes when I found 'em," he said.

It was the editorial Flem and Wes wrote in the saloon, entitled "Ode To Felix Kassner." The sheriff smiled. "If anything would draw Kassner out—that's it," he said.

Gregg shook his head. "He'd just call in Tyson who would hire some more gunslingers and we'd be right back where we were before."

The sheriff nodded. "If we could just figure a way to get them to do their own dirty work, we might nail both of them."

"It'll be damn near impossible to get Kassner to get his hands dirty, not as long as he's got Tyson. But we might be able to draw Tyson out."

The sheriff squinted through his glasses. "You mean through your friend Case?"

"You've heard then?"

"Hell boy, everybody in this part of the country has

117

heard by now. Most folks have been expecting it for several years now. A lively, goodlooking woman like LaVida ain't about to stay cooped up on that ranch for the rest of her life while her husband's spending half his time with other women.''

"Do you expect trouble?''

"Hard to say about a man like Tyson. He might just shrug it off. Then again, he might go off the loose end. How about Case? Is he serious, or just tomcatting?''

"Who knows what a poker player is thinking?''

"I figure he's serious.''

"Because of the flowers?''

The sheriff nodded. "A dozen roses would have said thanks. Sending her a wagon load like that, well, it seems to me he might be trying to provoke something.''

"You think he's baiting Tyson?''

"Could be.''

Gregg left the sheriff's office for Ryan's saloon where he found Case playing solitaire, flipping cards with quick, precise movements, as if practicing to keep his fingers nimble. His dark hair, streaked with gray, was trimmed neatly. His wide shoulders were erect. He wore a silk shirt, rare in Riley, and a vest that looked freshly pressed. He smoked a long black cigar.

Gregg took a seat across from him. "You look completely healed.''

"I had a great doctor.''

"It was the talk of the town how you went to every flower garden in Riley buying, begging, and stealing everything in bloom to send out to her.''

"No harm in a man thanking a lady who did him a favor.''

"Unless she happens to be married to Bert Tyson."

"What do you know about Bert Tyson?"

"Just that he washes Kassner's dirty linen."

"That tough, eh?"

"That tough."

Case shrugged. "I'm not looking for trouble."

Women rarely entered a saloon in Riley. When LaVida Tyson walked in, wearing a new red dress that hugged her trim figure like she was poured into it, the room became as quiet as a church. She walked straight to Case, signaling Gregg not to leave.

"I wanted to thank you in person, Case," she said.

"You're welcome."

"But why, Case? Why so dangerous a stunt?"

He looked into her eyes. "The stakes are high, LaVida. Things have a way of getting dangerous when the stakes are high."

"Haven't you won enough already?"

"All or nothing, LaVida. That's the way it's gotta be."

"Ten years ago I would have been flattered."

"And now?"

"All I see is bloodshed."

"It goes with the game sometimes."

LaVida nodded toward Gregg. "He might get involved too."

Case frowned. "How come? It's not his fight!"

"Jamie McPherson will insist on it. Bert won't make a move without him and Jamie considers you two a team."

"Thanks for the warning," said Gregg.

Case looked at Gregg. "Looks like I bring you nothing but trouble."

"I've got my own score to settle with Bert Tyson," replied Gregg. "If Jamie McPherson wants to stick his nose in it, that's his problem."

"Jamie's fast," said LaVida. "He's awful fast."

Gregg nodded. Case frowned, rubbing his jaw.

As soon as LaVida left Gregg rushed to the sheriff's office. "You were right," he said. "Case was baiting Bert Tyson. He's dead serious about that woman."

The sheriff shook his head. "Women!" He mumbled. "Show me one that feels scorned and I'll show you somebody who can wreck a whole damn town, just by wiggling her ass!"

Belle Colburn liked to have a man around, but not constantly. Flem Martin had sensed this in her the first day he saw her. That's why he loaned the school board a house for her and took her under his paternalistic wing. For the next three years he visited her frequently, to talk and drink. "If I was twenty years younger things would be very different between us," he'd chuckled. He pulled every trick in the book to get her safely and securely married.

"Why, Flem?" she once asked. "Why do you do so much for me?"

"Because you remind me of me when I was your age," he'd replied.

"You never married, except for a few months. Why should I?"

"Because people like us cause nothing but trouble as long as we're single."

"You've managed all right."

"I'm a man, Belle! It's different for a woman."

"I'll manage all right too. You'll see."

Belle had nothing against marriage. She just didn't

figure she was ready for it yet. She wanted a man occasionally—and then she wanted her life to be completely her own. The few men she met who appealed to her were delighted with the relationship she chose. It was like an offer of free milk without having to buy the cow. Those who wanted a more secure relationship and proposed marriage felt deceived when Belle turned them down—as if they had been tricked into donating milk to a bucket that wasn't theirs.

Some went into a rage when Belle suddenly decided to change men—threatening to shoot some imaginary rival. Others went into a deep depression, threatening suicide. Belle, never having experienced the torture of rejection, couldn't relate to their emotional outbursts. As a result they became a nuisance to her if they persisted in trying to make a permanent bond out of an occasional junction in bed, or they amused her if they vanished after an outburst of rage or self-pity.

Tom Macon, a smooth-talking salesman who traveled throughout the West, had more experience with women than any man Belle had ever met. He brought colorful gifts and he showered her with charm and poetic descriptions of her eyes, her face, her body. In bed he ranged from being so gentle she was hardly aware when he penetrated her body, to being so savage she woke up with bruises.

Tom Macon was not a bore—in bed or out.

He was, however, a complete phony—selling himself as he sold his bottles of a newly discovered cure for all bodily aches and pains. His poetic expressions, his gifts, even his carefully varied techniques in bed were all designed to impress—to elicit a certain reaction from Belle that gave him a sense of power over her, a feeling of conquest. Belle was quick to spot his phoniness, but his charm was such that she continued opening her door—and her legs—when he knocked. She would do this, willingly, until his charm wore itself out or until she found something better.

It wasn't until she decided to end their relationship that Belle learned something else about Tom Macon, something that surprised her. She approached the subject of termination very delicately, knowing how wild men could become when facing rejection.

"I hope we can always be very close friends, Tom," she had said, watching his eyes for signs of outrage or depression.

"Ouch!" he'd said, smiling.

"You understand then?"

"Nothing's permanent Belle—certainly not in my life."

She felt a sense of relief. "I meant that about being friends," she repeated.

"Who is it? Gregg Martin?"

"He's like his uncle in a lot of ways, and you know how I felt about Flem."

"I saw you in bed with him."

"You what?"

"The night Flem was killed. You didn't answer my knock. I went to see if you were asleep."

"Then you saw we were both fully dressed."

"I wondered if he'd suffered one of those horrible war wounds you hear about."

"Believe it or not, I wouldn't know."

"Not yet you mean." He paused, biting his lower lip. It was the first time Belle had ever seen pain in his eyes. "You've never been rejected, have you, Belle?"

"No, I guess I haven't."

"Scorned is the word they use when it happens to women. It's not a pleasant experience."

"I'm sorry."

"I feel sorry for the man that does reject you. You'll show him no mercy."

"What makes you think that?"

Tom smiled, not a phony smile to impress, but a real smile that came from within. "I know you, Belle Colburn," he said, kissing her cheek before walking out the door.

Tom Macon was not only an exciting lover and charming phony, he was also a good sport and unusually wise to the ways of women.

Moments after dismissing him she began getting ready for Gregg Martin. The few times they had been together since Flem's funeral, which they attended together, were stiff with polite correctness. She was now determined to change that. She met him in her usual skintight jeans and cotton shirt. "When are you going to start publishing the paper again?" she asked.

"I haven't decided yet to put one out."

She looked dumbfounded. "Why not?"

"I don't know anything about writing for a newspaper," he said.

"Then I'll teach you!"

"I'm not sure I'm cut out for it."

"I thought you were Flem's nephew?"

"You're more like him than I am. You want to put it out?"

"I could do most of the writing, but even Riley isn't ready yet for a woman editor."

"What would you write about?"

"My committees, of course, then little items about people that tell a lot to folks who know. I'd write an item about LaVida Tyson catching the afternoon train to Cheyenne to visit her sister. A lot of people would read a whole book into that."

"She didn't tell Case she was going."

"She wouldn't. It's not proper," replied Belle.

"What else?"

"I'd have to have an item about Harry Pratt spending several mornings building and painting two flower boxes instead of opening the saloon on time. Folks would get a big kick out of that."

"Why?"

"Because everybody knows he made one of them for Shelly Benson. They'll imagine all sorts of things."

"You're nothing but a gossip!"

"Gossip sells newspapers!"

"Is that all you'd write, gossip?"

"Oh no! I'd reprint stories out of other papers, go to the telegraph station and find out what news had come over the wire, talk to ranchers and miners when they come to town for supplies. There's a lot of places to get news. And then there's the fun stuff Flem used to write late at night, when he couldn't sleep."

"What kind of fun stuff?"

"Whatever came to his mind. He once wrote a front page story about a lion being loose in town, and about a murder in a mining shaft that didn't exist. Flem once did a whole series of stories about a bunch of scientists who were developing a machine that would crawl across the ocean floor to China."

"None of it true?"

"Not a word of it. The readers loved it! And then

there were Flem's famous editorials. Everybody read those."

Gregg dug in his pocket and pulled out the editorial Sheriff Richie had given him. "This was his last one," he said.

Belle read it, her eyes opening wide. "Sounds just like him," she said. "Just exactly like him! Are you going to publish it?"

"I don't know yet."

Gregg pulled out his pocket watch and frowned. The time had raced by. "I left Case in the saloon," he said. "He still isn't too strong and Bert Tyson might be gunning for him."

"I'm surprised Bert wouldn't hire a gunman for that."

"He couldn't get much satisfaction sending a hired gun to revenge his hurt pride. Looks to me like that's one job he'll have to do himself."

Belle nodded. "You seem to be making a habit of taking up for Case Anders." She said it with a trace of resentment.

He decided against mentioning Jamie McPherson. No sense complicating things.

"How about one short drink before you go?" she said brightly, disappearing into the kitchen before he could answer. When she returned with the drinks two buttons on her cotton shirt had mysteriously slipped loose. One flick of his finger and her breasts would come tumbling out like melons from a basket.

He instinctively wondered if she was sending him a message, then immediately kicked the thought out of his mind. He had no time for fun and games, not tonight. His eyes couldn't resist drifting to the deep cleavage, but he kept his mind on the business he was expecting—if not tonight, then some night soon.

He downed the drink. "Thanks," he said.

He refused to look at her eyes as he turned and abruptly departed. He didn't see the fury gleaming like hot steel, but he felt it. He felt her stare on the back of his head until he was out of sight. It felt like his head was about to be blown off.

It was quiet in Ryan's saloon. Case was playing low stakes draw poker with some ranchers at the rear table. He was facing the door. He looked tired.

Gregg took a hand. It was soon obvious the cards weren't running hot for anybody. The pot just moved from first one player to another, with nobody getting anywhere. Case managed to pull in the largest pots, but that was just because he was a little sharper than the others at building a pot when the cards were coming his way.

Sheriff Richie sat in for a few hands, then turned his cards over and went home. One of the ranchers started yawning a little after ten o'clock and it looked like the game was gonna break up. Gregg hoped so. He wanted to get a good night's sleep. Case looked like he could use one too.

It was ten-thirty on the nose when Bert Tyson walked in. He stood in the doorway a second, just staring at Case. Then he went to the bar and ordered a whiskey which he carried to a table. He sat alone, facing the poker players. His eyes never left Case.

Jamie McPherson came in next. He stood at the bar. Then a third one came, Lew Rollins. Rollins stayed near the door. All three of them were watching Case.

McPherson, leaning against the bar, shouted across the room to Bert Tyson. "Mess a flowers came to the ranch yesterday," he said. "I fed 'em to the hogs."

The two ranchers turned their cards over and left the game for the bar. Gregg scooted his chair around to where he was a few yards to one side of Case, facing the front door, just like Case was.

"This isn't your fight," whispered Case.

"What fight?" asked Gregg.

"They made the hogs sick," said McPherson. "I thought you oughta know, Bert."

Bert Tyson kept looking at Case. "Wonder who'd wanta make a bunch a hogs sick?" asked McPherson. "A man that would do that is about as dirty a low-down snake as ever crawled under a rock." He began bouncing on his toes, letting off nervous energy. While everybody was looking at McPherson, Bert pulled iron under the table and aimed it at Case Anders.

Gregg, looking straight at Jamie, slowly stood. He didn't have any nervous energy that had to be let off. He didn't bounce or make a single move that wasn't necessary. He just stood, eyeing Jamie the whole time. When Jamie looked at Case, Gregg's eyes glanced to Harry Pratt who began edging slowly down the bar, away from Jamie and toward Lew Rollins. When Harry was almost opposite Rollins he reached under the counter, then looked at Gregg and nodded slightly.

Case sat motionless, his hands in his lap, under the table. In his right hand was a small derringer, aimed straight at Bert Tyson.

"How about my buying you a drink, Mr. Tyson, and we talk this over," said Case.

"I don't drink with tinhorns!" replied Tyson.

Jamie and Gregg eyeballed each other, each getting a feel of the other's strength, the other's speed, the other's determination—just by looking. Case looked from one to the other, feeling the tension mount between them in the silence. He couldn't let that go on. This wasn't their fight.

Case drew his hands from under the table. His derringer was aimed straight at Jamie McPherson.

Bert Tyson brought his Colt from under the table, aiming it straight at Case.

Tyson looked at Lew Rollins, who looked fearfully at Harry Pratt. Harry took his hand from under the counter. In it was a .44 caliber dragoon revolver, big enough to drop a running buffalo. It was aimed straight at Lew Rollins' gut.

Nobody said a word, nor was there any need to. It was all in the open now, for everybody to see. If Jamie or Lew Rollins went for their guns they'd be dropped before they could touch pistol grips. Bert Tyson would get his chance to fill Case with lead, but it would cost him both of his men and the odds were high that Gregg and Harry Pratt would catch Tyson in a crossfire after he got off one, maybe two slugs into Case.

That was a big price to pay, much bigger than Bert Tyson had counted on—much bigger than Bert Tyson wanted to pay. He holstered his gun, stood, and backed toward the door.

Jamie kept his eyes on Gregg. "I want a piece of him!" he screamed.

"You'll have yer chance," said Tyson. "But not tonight."

CHAPTER 10

Millie Anderson was the kind of widow folks knew about, but never talked about. People liked her and accepted her, that's why. She had flaming red hair which she brushed into all kinds of wild patterns, depending on her mood of the moment, and enormous bosoms that attracted male eyes because they were constantly threatening to spill out of her dresses.

It was her smile, which she lavished on anybody and everybody, and her generous nature that made folks accept her, and pretend she didn't keep girls handy for guests in her hotel or carry on with a select few of the guests herself, when she had the urge.

Millie spent most of her time at the front desk, welcoming guests as they registered, making sure they were satisfied with their rooms, keeping a sharp eye on the hired help and visiting with anybody who happened to stop in.

When Gregg checked in, Millie immediately took him under her wing, like a mother hen. Gregg thought she did it because his uncle was a permanent guest at the hotel and she wanted to keep the Martin family happy for business reasons. Later, when he was cleaning out Flem's room, he began to suspect there was more to Millie's mother henning him than just business. In one of Flem's dresser drawers Gregg found a neatly folded, silk negligee heavily laced with the same perfume Millie used. Gregg also noticed several strands of long red hair clinging to a nightshirt his uncle had left under the bed.

Gregg never mentioned his finds to Millie, but when he started calling her Aunt Millie she gave one of those deep warm chuckles that seemed to say she knew he'd learned something from somewhere, and she was glad.

She didn't chuckle when she heard about the near showdown at Ryan's saloon. She marched into Gregg's room early the next morning and hauled him out of bed. "You gotta practice with your shooting iron," she said. "Jamie McPherson is a hotheaded little punk and he'll come a gunning for ya one a these days. Mind my words!"

"I hear he's pretty fast."

"He is that!"

Speed wasn't Gregg's strongest suit. He was an excellent shot, but his moves were usually calculated, which denied him the speed that a man has when he reacts strictly from instinct. Millie was right. He needed practice.

"Sheriff Richie's waiting in the lobby," she said. "He knows more about guns, and killings for that matter, than anybody in this part of the country."

Every morning for the next week Gregg and the sheriff spent two hours just outside of town with pistols and tin cans. Richie had the patience of a school marm explaining the final details of what he called "man shooting." But after he explained something once his patience ended.

"Stop squeezing that grip!" he shouted. "Hold it firm, just like you're shaking hands with it. That's it ... Now you gotta make up your mind about your trigger finger, Gregg. If you want to use just the tip of your finger, fine. If you want to use the entire first joint, that's fine too. But you gotta be consistent. If you switch from one to the other your aim will be off ... Keep your head up, up, goddammit! Raise your weapon to your eye, not the other way around ... Once again with your breathing now. Take a normal breath, exhale half of it, hold it, fire, exhale ... once more, breath normal, exhale half a breath, hold it, fire, exhale ... keep it up until it's second nature. Good, excellent!"

At night Gregg carried a ball of leather, squeezing it to strengthen his finger muscles. At Richie's insistence, he wore an old horseshoe wrapped like a bracelet around his wrist. The extra weight helped him steady his shooting arm when aiming.

In the afternoons Gregg practiced alone, learning to keep his weight evenly divided between his two feet, to bend his knees as he drew, to lean slightly forward, keeping his arm and hand in a straight line.

He was surprised at how quickly it all became second nature to him, but he was under no illusions that he was a great shooter. His accuracy was good. He knew he could remain calm and his concentration would be good. He had learned those things in the war, and they came back to him. But he also knew he was not as fast as Jamie McPherson. His speed was getting steadily better, but he concentrated so intently on accuracy there was a limit to how fast he could increase his speed. He knew there wasn't enough time for him to get fast enough to beat Jamie McPherson.

Millie kept a close eye on him. "Keep practicing," she said. "Flem would be proud of the way you're doing."

"I can't make it on speed," he said. "I'll just have to stay alert and catch his mistake."

"What mistake?" asked Millie.

"He'll make one. Most folks do. I'll have to be on the lookout for it."

Gregg had stopped at the front desk to see if he had any mail. Millie, glancing over his shoulder, suddenly opened her eyes wide with fear. Gregg knew who caused it, before he turned around.

There, in the middle of the lobby, hardly ten yards away, stood Jamie, eyeballing him exactly as he had in Ryan's saloon. Jamie was bouncing on the balls of his feet, clenching and relaxing his fists which he held above his waist.

Lew Rollins stood in the doorway. Lew was wearing two guns this time, both low. They were for show, for bluff. Nobody could draw very fast from holsters hanging that low. They were good for intimidating people though. Just the sight of those two guns, grips out like they were, made most folks want to give Lew

Rollins a wide berth.

Jamie had one gun, resting high on his waist. He had an opentoed holster that glistened from fresh wax. There was no chance of a gunsight catching leather to slow his draw. A gentle nudge was all it took to spring iron from that heat-hardened holster.

"We got some unfinished business," said Jamie.

Gregg quickly calculated the odds and decided he was holding a bad hand. Like most cautious men, he carried only five rounds in the six chambers of his gun, leaving the firing pin on an empty chamber. The odds were heavy that Jamie took no such precaution. In addition, Jamie had planned the meeting, and was ready for it. Gregg had been thinking of having dinner with Belle. He wasn't mentally ready for a showdown with anybody.

Steady boy, he cautioned himself. Watch their eyes. Watch for the mistake. They'll make one. Everybody makes at least one. Wait and watch for it. Steady. Cunning, that's what it takes when you're outgunned. Cunning, not courage. Watch for the mistake. Let him be the one with courage. Let him do the charging, the strutting. You just wait, and watch. Steady boy. Steady.

"He spoke to you, boy," said Lew Rollins, letting everybody know he was part of this. Lew had a low, hoarse voice, like he'd swallowed too much trail dust.

Gregg ignored him. His eyes never left Jamie. If Jamie made a play it would show in his eyes first. Gregg didn't intend to miss the first signal, perhaps the last signal.

It was coming. Gregg could feel it. It was coming and Jamie was ready—eager was a better word. Jamie must have been working himself up to it for days. His eyes glared like the eyes of a wild animal. He was right on the edge, ready to explode into action.

It was suddenly clear to Gregg that there would be no turning back this time, no sudden show of force or cunning that would change Jamie's mind. He'd worked himself up for this moment, and now he was gonna see it through. The only question was, who was gonna trigger it—Gregg or Jamie. Gregg decided he'd better.

"Okay McPherson, crap or climb off the pot!" he barked, his muscles tensing. His voice, harsh and sudden, caused Jamie's eyes to open in shock for an instant, then harden into an instinctive squint. It was the early warning signal Gregg was expecting. Both men started simultaneously for their holsters.

Just as their hands darted for leather Millie Anderson screamed. It was more than just a woman's scream. It was a Millie Anderson scream; a loud, ear-piercing scream several octaves above the scream Millie used to fetch hired help from the other end of the building. It was a scream that made ears hurt and hearts skip beats. It was a familiar scream to Gregg Martin. Had he thought about it, he would have expected it. The instant he heard it he instinctively knew what it was and why she did it. Millie always screamed when something upset her. Gregg had heard her scream, to a lesser degree, many times.

It was not a familiar sound to Jamie McPherson. He didn't even know what it was at first, the scream was so sudden and so earshattering. He had started his move when the sound hit him, and there was no stopping his hand. His hand touched the gun butt and he gripped, lifting. But the shrill scream, like a crash of lightning, splintered his concentration and his timing. His eyes darted instinctively toward her. Even his head turned slightly, interfering with the smooth flow of his hand to his weapon. He was distracted only long enough to see Millie's hands cover her mouth and the fear in her eyes. When his eyes bounced back to Gregg and he felt his weapon in his hand it was too late. Millie's scream had done its work. He got off the first shot, but his aim was off, ever so slightly.

Gregg's eyes never left Jamie. His hand moved swiftly and smoothly to his holster. He clicked off the empty shot as he drew, then blasted straight at Jamie's heart when the barrel was level. He was supremely confident his shot had hit its mark, but he squeezed off another one anyhow, just in case. Then he threw a wild one in Lew's direction, hoping only to fluster the big man with his two low hung pistols.

Jamie was blasted backward, but his pistol was still in his hand, pointed forward. Gregg fired his fourth shot right into Jamie's face then threw another quick one toward Lew, catching his right shoulder and knocking a gun from his right hand.

To everybody's surprise the wound hardly phased the big man. He smiled. It was a weird, a grotesque smile, but a smile nevertheless. Blood began crawling out of the hole in his right arm, which hung limp at his side. With his left hand he slowly aimed his second pistol right at Gregg's face. His smile grew and a deep chuckle rumbled in his throat. "You wanta pray a little first!" he asked.

Gregg stared at him, as he had earlier stared at Jamie, then raised his pistol, closing an eye, aiming straight at Lew's head. "Do you?" he asked.

"You got off five shots. I counted em! You're empty!"

"I'll give you a count of three to move out, Lew."

"You're bluffing. Your gun's empty!" Lew looked at his former boss and could hardly recognize him. A bullet had split Jamie's lower lip, smashed his upper lip, ripped his nose to one side and cut a bloody furrow between his eyes, leaving one eyeball hanging to one side.

"You're crazy!" shouted Lew.

"One!"

"You ain't the type to walk around with a fully loaded gun. It's empty now, and you know it!"

"Two!"

"Crazy! You're—"

"THR-RRR—"

Lew ran out the door, holstering his gun as he went. Gregg walked to the door and watched as Lew leaped into his saddle and made dust getting out of town.

"Was he right?" asked Millie.

"About what?"

"Are you holding an empty gun?"

Millie watched him disappear up the stairs, then looked at the remains of Jamie McPherson, then shook her head. "Yeah," she said softly, to no one in particular. "I'd bet this hotel on it."

Gregg went to his room and sat staring at the empty pistol. Case would have been proud of the bluff he'd pulled. He was proud of it himself. But he felt a knot in his gut when he thought about what could have happened.

The curtains swayed gently when the door behind

him opened and then softly closed. It was Etta, the new girl. Gregg had first seen her the previous morning, bending over a bed to change sheets. He'd stopped in the hall and was staring when Millie walked by. She flashed her most lecherous grin. "You like that, do you?" she asked.

There was no sense trying to hide anything from Millie. "It's very nice from this side," he said.

Now Etta was standing beside his bed, looking at him. Her face wasn't as exciting as her backside had been. Her eyes squinted, as if she was nearsighted, and her mouth covered the bottom half of her face. "Millie said you wanted something," she said.

"What?"

Etta grinned, displaying a mouth of big teeth. "She didn't say. Just something. I thought maybe your bed wasn't made up to suit you."

"The bed's all right."

"Everybody's talking about you downstairs."

"What are they saying?"

"You're some kinda hero!"

"That and two bits will get me a good drink of whiskey."

"If I was you I'd be so fidgety I couldn't sit still."

"I'm trying to relax."

"Want some help?"

"All right."

Etta took a pillow off the bed and put it at his feet, then sat on it. She unbuckled his pants as casually as opening a sack of flour and began gently massaging his privates. "I'll have you settled in no time," she promised. She bent forward, running the tip of her pink tongue over the head of his tool.

"I'm getting more relaxed already," said Gregg, as his cock leaped up, only to disappear inside her huge mouth. He worried about her large teeth until he felt her tongue cover one side of his shaft and the inside of her cheeks begin to constrict rhythmically. She not only liked her work, but was obviously experienced at it. His tool grew, and then throbbed.

She lifted her head, then lowered it, then lifted it again—slowly at first. Her tongue eased around and around, then her head came up and went down again. He felt a light suction which slowly grew in strength until he felt unable to pull it out of her mouth—even if he wanted to. He didn't. All he wanted to do was lean back and enjoy. Soon he felt like an oil well, just before it blew.

He could have sworn there was an explosion when he came, strong enough to knock her head back, or at least to cause her to gag. He was amazed that her tongue kept moving, the sucking action continued with the same rhythmic regularity. Her massive mouth absorbed it all. She stayed on him until he began to recede inside himself. Then she got a towel and cleaned him as she would a baby.

"Relaxed now?" she asked.

"Perfectly."

"That's what Red Fred used to say."

"Red Fred?"

"He had red hair and his name was Fred."

"It figures."

"Red Fred used to say my mouth could give him a better night's sleep than a dozen pussies."

"Who was Red Fred?"

"My stepfather."

"He raised you well."

She laughed. "Red Fred didn't raise me. He didn't marry Maw until I was grown. He said he wanted to marry me, but—"

"But what?"

"Maw owned the ranch."

"Did you leave home to get away from him?"

"In a way. Maw chased me off. She said me and Red Fred hit it off too well."

"I can see why."

"You sure your bed was made up to suit you?"

"Positive."

"I wonder what Millie thought you wanted."

"Damned if I know."

She carefully replaced the pillow on the bed. "If you think of anything you need, just give me a yell. Millie says I should see that you're comfortable."

"Good ole Millie!"

After Etta left Gregg thought of Belle. It was silly the way she was being so cold every time they happened to pass in town. It chewed at his insides. The colder she looked, the more painful the chewing felt. He decided to do something about that coldness.

He would resume publication of the *Gazette.*

CHAPTER 11

As soon as Congress officially established the Wyoming Territory Felix Kassner's name became publicly discussed as a possible territorial governor. Riley became feverish over the possibility. Kassner had been feverish from the beginning, which continued to amaze Bert Tyson who still considered the job just a little short of ridiculous.

He was flabbergasted when he saw how the leading citizens of Riley reacted. Everybody who was anybody seemed hell-bent and determined to be able to say he knew the governor. People started pouring by the ranch to offer their congratulations, long before there was anything to congratulate.

If Kassner had been a popular man it would have been different, but he wasn't popular, nor did he deserve to be in Tyson's view. He had never done a damn thing for anybody in his life, except for Felix Kassner, and he had little patience with and no love for people. He even went out of his way to make his business associates uncomfortable when they visited him in his study. He didn't want them taking too much of his time.

Still, people poured in to pay homage to the little man, to bow and scrape before him. Kassner accepted it all with an air of arrogant indifference, as if it were his destiny to rule and by paying homage to him his subjects were merely acknowledging the inevitable.

Tyson accepted it all with a shrug. It was the first time he'd ever seen people react to what they perceived to be power. The more successful they were, the more wealth and prestige they had, the more eager they seemed to be to get close to power, to be associated with it—which is to say, to kiss Kassner's behind.

In no time Kassner began reacting with more and more of a sense of superiority. He seemed to hold his head a little more erect when greeting a well-wisher and he moved with a little more majesty. He reminded Tyson of a stage player the way his gestures became more and more exaggerated, and finally when he began acting somewhat bored with it all. "I need to get some air," Kassner said one morning. "We shall inspect the ranch, Mr. Tyson," he said.

That began a regular morning ride over various sections of the ranch, checking water holes, the condition of cattle, and watching the men perform their various chores. Tyson wasn't sure whether Kassner took the rides for the air, the exercise, or just to keep well-wishers waiting uncomfortably at the ranch for his return. Whatever the reason, Tyson welcomed the break. He felt more comfortable in the saddle than sitting around the ranch.

That is, he enjoyed it until the morning rides began taking on the overtures of some kind of a military inspection tour. Kassner began eyeballing the men as if he were examining their dress and the way they stood or sat in a saddle. Those who snapped to attention and gave a slight nod of respect, something similar to a salute, were rewarded with a terse smile from Kassner and a crisp wave of his riding crop. Those who looked up when he approached, then went back to stretching fence wire, slapping a branding iron on a calf, or herding some strays back to the main body received cold frowns.

The men made a joke of it among themselves, often stopping everything they were doing and making wildly exaggerated gestures of standing rigidly at attention until they received their smile and the wave of the riding crop. They would look at Kassner like little puppies who wanted only a chance to lick the hand of their master. After he was out of sight they'd roll over laughing.

It was no joke with Kassner.

Bert Tyson became more and more bored with it all. He occupied himself with ranch business as much as he could, but Kassner liked to have him nearby when there were visitors, and that made Tyson restless. He had to have some diversion, which meant he needed a woman.

LaVida was still in Cheyenne. He began thinking more and more of Shelly.

Gregg Martin noticed the sudden excitement that rippled through the business community when Kassner's name began appearing in eastern papers as a possible choice for governor. He was puzzled by it at first, but little by little began to accept it. He realized from the beginning that it wasn't Kassner's popularity that created the excitement. It was the fact that his appointment might have a beneficial effect on business in Riley.

Theodore Bilkins, president of the Riley National Bank, seemed particularly excited over the turn of events. Bilkins was a mild-mannered little man who liked crisp white shirts and gray suits. Some said he wasn't strong enough to rope a cow so he had no choice but to push a pencil.

"Something like this could put Riley on the map," said Bilkins excitedly. "It will bring tourists, new business, industrial opportunities! We must all get solidly behind Mr. Kassner and do what we can to assure his appointment. If it's not him, the President will appoint some friend who has probably never been in the Territory—and might not even bother to come!"

Bilkins had a point, but Gregg Martin had an editorial his uncle had written and the more talk he heard about Kassner's appointment, the more urgently he wanted to print it.

After he decided to resume publication of the *Gazette* Belle's coldness thawed considerably, but she kept her shirt buttoned to the top and every time Gregg looked like he was going to suggest that she loosen a button or two a glaze of icy anger came over her eyes, freezing him in his tracks. Still, friendly talk about the paper was better than no talk at all.

"There's no question in my mind that Uncle Flem knew this was going to happen," he said. "That's why he wrote that editorial."

"Wonder how he knew?" asked Belle.

"Maybe Wes Darby found out."

"A lot of people will be down on you if you print it."

Gregg smiled. "That's better than having Uncle Flem's ghost haunting me the rest of my life."

The *Gazette* only had two full-time employees besides Gregg. There was Bellevue, who had been around a long time, and a printer. The printer slot changed every few months. The printer left, without notice, just as Gregg decided to publish a copy of the *Gazette.*

That's when he decided to become a printer.

Gregg got the set of instructions on how to handle the Washington Hand Press and practiced until he was confident he could print a thousand copies of the *Gazette* himself—and Bellevue could keep from getting too far behind with the printing orders they had.

Belle wrote most of the copy. Gregg and Bellevue worked far into the night getting it ready for the final printing. He centered Flem's editorial on the front page, with a solid black border around it.

"That isn't where you run editorials," said Belle. "Look at any of the other papers."

Gregg smiled. "Let the other papers look at us," he replied.

Anybody who glanced at any portion of the *Gazette* couldn't help but see Flem Martin's last editorial.

Sheriff Richie came to the Gazette building just as Gregg was pulling off the first copy. He looked grave.

"I think you should wait a bit," he said. "It's gonna mean trouble, Gregg, trouble like you've never seen before!"

"I've already waited too long," replied Gregg. "Flem planned to publish this early, before all the talk started about what a great thing it would be for Riley if Kassner made it as governor. I guess he figured to end Kassner's chances before folks got excited. I can't wait any longer."

"Folks would have expected something like this from Flem. They would expect it and accept it. I'm not so sure it'll be the same, coming from you, Gregg."

"What's the difference?"

"They knew Flem stood for a certain way of life, a certain way of looking at things. Some agreed and some didn't. Most didn't, if the truth were known. But they understood him and they accepted him as one a them. They don't know you, except that you're Flem's nephew."

"They'll get to know me."

The sheriff rubbed his slightly whiskered jaw. This wasn't easy for him. "They're getting to know you already, or they think they do. They figure you got a fiery temper, just like your uncle. But there the resemblance stops, in their eyes. You see, Gregg, you came to town with a gambler who some folks think tried to take advantage of another man's wife. Then when trouble came you stood with the gambler, not the husband. A lot of folks who don't know the whole story think it should have been the other way around. You gunned down Jamie McPherson. You and I know how it happened, but a lot of folks don't know anything except the fact that you gunned him down. In their eyes you're little more than a fast gun." The sheriff glanced at the editorial. "Now they're gonna say you're sticking your nose into who gets appointed governor of this Territory—something a lot of folks figure is simply none of your business." He looked up into Gregg's eyes. "It all adds up to a hell of a misunderstanding, Gregg, but it's something we have to live with, we gotta face. This editorial can turn on you, turn on you bad."

Gregg chewed his lower lip. A lot of what the sheriff said made sense to him. "I appreciate your coming by," he said.

"But you're going to print it anyhow, is that it?"

Gregg nodded. "That's it."

Gregg worked until almost daybreak finishing the printing. He bundled twenty papers for the morning train. They were addressed to Senators and Congressmen in Washington. He figured at least one would find its way to the White House.

He put a pile on the imposing stone for Bellevue to address and mail when he had time. He piled most of the rest on the front counter where the delivery boy would find them and make his deliveries. Then he put a bundle under his arm and headed for the hotel. The night man wasn't sleeping, which surprised Gregg. He was standing wide awake behind the counter.

"Bet ya didn't get the latest news in that paper," he said.

"What latest news?" asked Gregg.

"Bert Tyson came to town, got all liquored up and took Shelly Bensen with him when he left—kicking and screaming they say!"

Bert Tyson had a hangover and the scratches on the side of his face burned when he shaved, but he figured he was in a hell of a lot better shape than Kassner. He seriously thought the little man would have a stroke before he could finish reading the latest copy of the Riley *Gazette.* Kassner's face flushed a deep red. His eyes glared. He gulped air in deep, gasping breaths, then broke into a brisk pace around his desk. "Treason!" he screamed. "This is treason!"

Tyson squirmed in the uncomfortable chair. It was just another issue of a newspaper as far as he was concerned. He never had been able to understand why people got so stirred up over things that appeared in newspapers. Everybody knew they were a pack of lies. "Theodore Bilkins is waiting to see you about it," he said.

Kassner continued to pace furiously. "That paper must be destroyed!" he screamed. "It must be wiped off the face of the earth!"

"I can get some men and—"

"Get 'em! Get a lot of men!"

"Will do."

Kassner circled the room, glanced at the opened paper on his desk and circled it again. Then he stopped behind his desk and took a deep breath. "I must control myself, Mr. Tyson," he said. "This situation calls for clear thinking."

"That's what I was thinking, Mr. Kassner. No time to go off half-cocked."

"Another issue must be printed, immediately. There must be a retraction. We will destroy it later, but first we must conquer it!"

Tyson understood only half of what he heard. He

nodded his head, agreeing with all of it.

Kassner's color returned to near normal. His breathing relaxed. "Find enough men to take the paper, to take the town if necessary! In the meantime, send in Mr. Bilkins. He might very well be our first line of attack!"

Theodore Bilkins was extremely agitated when he entered Kassner's study. "I hope you realize that the *Gazette*does not speak for the business community of Riley," he said. "All of us are just as upset over this outrage as you are. I personally sent ten wires to Washington as soon as I read it—endorsing your appointment and denouncing the Riley *Gazette* There are dozens of others who will do the same. Young Martin is not going to get away with this!"

Bilkins' agitation seemed to relax Kassner, who sat behind his desk perfectly still, listening intently. The only sign of nervousness he exhibited was an occasional drumming of his manicured fingers on the desk top.

"I appreciate your support, Mr. Bilkins," he said calmly. "But I'm afraid a few wires won't suffice. My political advisors in Washington inform me that one editorial upsets politicians more than a hundred telegrams from what they call special interest groups."

"What more can I do, Mr. Kassner?"

"You might help convince Mr. Martin that it is to his advantage to publish a retraction."

Bilkins appeared shocked at the idea. "I'm afraid that will be . . . if he's any kin to Flem he . . . I never heard of the *Gazette* changing its mind, once something is in print . . ."

"This is now a business matter, Mr. Bilkins—pure

and simple. It might be possible to convince Mr. Martin that the position he has taken is bad for business—very bad. Is there an outstanding mortgage on his building?"

"I'm afraid not. Flem Martin hated the thought of debt."

"How about his advertisers?"

"Most of them would be willing to refuse to advertise, for a limited period of time. They are strongly against his position in this matter. But I'm not sure that would have the desired impact, Mr. Kassner. The paper doesn't make that much from advertising. Most of Martin's business is in printing."

"Is there another printer in Riley?"

"The closest one is in Bensenville. His rates are higher and his printing isn't as good. Martin gets a lot of business from Bensenville businessmen!"

Kassner looked angry over the response. He leaped out of his chair, his face once again flushing a deep red. "I don't think you're getting the message, Mr. Bilkins! Let me put it this way. If you want the funds I have deposited in your bank to remain in your bank and if you want territorial funds left in my charge, in the event I'm appointed governor, to be deposited in your bank—you better damn well find some way to put a financial squeeze on Gregg Martin! Is that clear?"

"I, I—"

"Is that clear, Mr. Bilkins?"

"Yes, sir. Perfectly clear!"

"Excellent. Good day, sir!"

Theodore Bilkins was trembling when he left Kassner's study.

Kassner was smiling when Tyson came back in. "I think we have the full support of the businessmen in Riley," he said. "You won't have to get enough men to take the whole town. Just enough to take the *Gazette*"

"That'll be a lot easier." Bert had a worried look on his face. "Did you send for the sheriff?" he asked.

"No."

"He's heading this way."

Kassner walked to the window. "I wonder what's on his mind?"

"No telling," replied Tyson, looking even more worried.

Kassner got a slight gleam in his eye, then he smiled. "Send him in the instant he gets here," he said. "He just might be able to help us."

Tyson met Richie at the front door. "Mr. Kassner wants to see you," he said.

"I've come to see Shelly."

"Why don't you talk to Mr. Kassner while I try to find her."

Richie paused, staring hard at Tyson. "Is she all right?"

"Of course she's all right! She's probably in the kitchen, cleaning something."

"I want to see her before I leave."

"Sure, sheriff."

Sheriff Richie reacted to Kassner's presence differently from the many other visitors. He didn't like the hard-backed chair he was offered, so he stood. When he got tired of standing he sat on the edge of Kassner's desk. In either case he towered over his host, which made Kassner uncomfortable. His general attitude also made Kassner ill at ease. Richie didn't seem to realize he was in the presence of the next governor of the Territory.

"If I'm appointed I suppose that will make me your commanding officer," said Kassner.

"I ain't appointed, Mr. Kassner. I'm elected by the voters. They're the only superior officers I know anything about."

"Of course. But you do recognize the necessity of our working together, in a spirit of cooperation, don't you?"

"That I do."

"I understand you're a friend of Gregg Martin's."

"That's right."

Kassner threw his copy of the *Gazette* on the desk, his eyes flashing. "Have you seen this?"

"Everybody in town's seen it by now."

"Well? What do you think of it?"

"I think that's between you and him."

"I understand he might listen to you, if he'll listen to anybody."

"Depends on what I tell him."

Kassner walked to the window, then turned slowly. "I want you to tell him to run a retraction," he said.

Richie almost laughed at the idea. "I don't tell folks how to run their business, unless they're breaking the law."

Kassner walked back to his desk unperturbed, like a businessman about to play a trump card in negotiating a delicate business deal. "Riley is a nice, peaceful little town, and your job is to keep it that way. Isn't that right, sheriff?"

Richie nodded, eyeing him carefully, waiting.

Kassner's eyes suddenly became hard, even vicious, glaring with determination. He spoke between clenched teeth. "If there is no retraction within three days, Riley will no longer be a quiet, peaceful town, sheriff. You have my word on that!"

"I don't take to being leaned on, Mr. Kassner. I don't take to that at all." Sheriff Richie walked out of Kassner's study, closing the door softly behind him.

There was gonna be trouble. He was convinced of that now. But then he'd figured it from the very beginning. He wished Gregg hadn't run that damn editorial! Richie could do without this kind of trouble.

He went to the kitchen, looking for Shelly. He found Bert Tyson pouring himself a cup of coffee. "Where is she?" he asked.

Bert shrugged. "Couldn't find her, sheriff."

The sheriff looked out the back door at the clump of cabins. "Which one's hers?"

"Last one on the left."

Sheriff Richie strolled to Shelly's cabin, knocked several times, then tried the door. It was locked. She wasn't at the stables or anywhere in the main house. He could feel Tyson's eyes on him the whole time he looked.

"Tell her I stopped in to say hello," he said, then headed back toward town.

As soon as he was clear of the ranch, Richie left the trail and doubled back. He circled around to the Marble Creek trail, then headed back toward Kassner's ranch. He figured he would make it before dark, which meant he might be spotted by Bert Tyson, or one of the ranch hands. He just hoped he could get to Shelly before they interfered.

He hadn't gone far when he heard hoof beats ahead, coming toward him. He pulled off the trail, behind a thicket, and waited. Whoever it was, was coming fast. He took his pistol out of the holster and spun the cylinder around a notch putting a live cartridge under the firing pin. When he recognized the lone rider he spun it back and replaced his gun in his holster.

"Why'd you hide from me back there?" he asked.

"Bert thought it best," replied Shelly. She had a swollen eye and there was a small red line at the corner of her lip where it had been split. "I figured you'd come back. That's why I come out to meet you."

"You wanta go back to town with me?"

"No."

"No harm will come to you, Shelly. I guarantee it. We can go straight from here, right now, or we can ride back to the ranch and get your things. Either way you want it. You'll be all right."

"You remind me of Dora. She keeps saying I'll be all right."

"She's staying with Belle Colburn."

"I figured she would. Belle's a good woman. She loves Dora and can do a lot for her—a lot more than I can."

"Did he force you to go back, against your will?"

Shelly chuckled. "Life forced me back, Boyd, I have no money, no land, no family. My youth was spent on the line. I'm lucky to have somebody like Bert Tyson, and you know it."

"You didn't get that black eye and split lip discussing your situation with him, Shelly."

She chuckled again. "He had a little too much to drink and lost his temper. Men do that sometimes, particularly with women like me." She paused, laughing again. "Hell, sheriff, you don't think this is the first black eye I've ever had, do you?"

"I reckon not."

"And it won't be the last either!"

"Why'd you hide from me, Shelly?"

"Same reason I rode out here to meet you. I don't want any more trouble. I made my bed, sheriff—a long time ago. I made it and now I have to sleep in it. I wanted Dora to have a chance for something different, some'in better. Well, she's got it now. She can make it, with some help from Belle. She don't need me anymore. She sure don't need me hanging around her neck, holding her back."

"She don't look at it that way, Shelly."

"It's not important how she looks at it. The important thing is, she's got a chance, without me holding her back, and I aim to see that she takes it."

"I can't see you staying with Bert."

"I could do a lot worse."

"He'll drop you, Shelly. Just as soon's he sees something on the line that shines up to him, makes him feel young and full of vinegar, he'll be moving her into your spot and putting you out on the trail. I've seen him do it before."

"I'll have to cross that bridge when I get to it, sheriff."

They heard hoof beats behind them, faint at first, but they got steadily louder. The sheriff's first thought was that Bert had followed him, dropping back when he saw for certain where he was headed, and was now closing the gap.

"I left Bert at the ranch," said Shelly. "It has to be

somebody else."

"They must not want to be seen, taking this back trail. We better get behind those thickets until we know who it is."

The lone rider was not experienced with horse flesh, nor was he riding a very strong looking animal. But what he lacked in ability and horse flesh he more than made up for in sheer determination. Harry Pratt, one boot hanging loose from the stirrup, daylight flashing between the saddle and his bottom as he bounced painfully, was belting his mount forward with all the energy he could pour into a thin switch and anxious shouts of "Hi, hi! Gidup there, George, gidup!"

"Hold on, podner!" said Sheriff Richie, smiling as he trotted on to the trail, holding his hand up in a gesture of peace.

Harry almost fell off coming to a stop. His face was red and he was panting as if he'd been doing the running. When he saw Shelly his eyes lit up and his whole face broke into a smile. "You two come all this way just to welcome me?" he joked.

"What are you doing way out here?" asked Shelly, as if afraid of hearing his answer.

"I heard Bert Tyson dragged you back here. I come to see for myself."

Shelly's breath caught in her throat. She bit her lower lip until she almost split it. "Bert didn't drag me anywhere," she said. "I came on my own."

Harry looked sadly disappointed. "Is that a fact sheriff?"

"That's what she says," he replied.

Harry looked at Shelly, until she finally turned her head. "You go on back to the saloon, where you belong, Harry Pratt," she said.

"Dora said you didn't want to come back out here?"

"Dora's just a child. What does she know?"

"But she said—"

"She dreams things. Haven't you ever known a young girl before, Harry Pratt? They dream things, all of 'em do! You go now! I've got some business with the sheriff, then I have to get back to the ranch, where I belong."

Harry Pratt's face was lower than the shoes on his horse as he jerked his steed clumsily around and headed back toward town.

He was no sooner out of sight than tears collected in Shelly's eyes. The sheriff saw them and looked away. "If you want to go with him I'll do my best to protect him," he said. "I'll do everything the law allows."

"Bert would gun him down in a minute, and you know it."

"There's other towns."

"None far enough." She threw her head up, her eyes sparkling with fresh tears. "You're right about Bert Tyson. He'll move another poor wench in my place one a these days and I'll be out in the cold. But until then I'm his property and he'll kill anybody or anything that threatens to take his property."

"Harry's a good man," said the sheriff.

"The kindest I've ever known. You ride back with him, you hear? He's liable to get thrown off that old nag and break a leg or something."

The sheriff nodded. "I'll look after him."

"Tell Dora not to worry. I made my bed. It's only right I sleep in it. I'll be all right. You tell her that."

"I'll tell her."

The sheriff raced down the trail until he caught up with Harry Pratt. They didn't say a word as they walked slowly back to town.

CHAPTER 12

It was a beautiful day for a picnic. Belle and Dora, tired of being cooped up in Belle's small house, hummed as they stacked the food into a basket and covered it with a tea cloth. Both of them felt like they'd worried about things they couldn't do anything about until there just wasn't any sense worrying any more. That's why they'd suggested a picnic. Now that they were actually going, they felt lighthearted, almost giddy. They were packed and ready long before Gregg was due to pick them up in the wagon.

Case Anders was to come later on horseback, to make sure nobody followed them. It would be a miracle if some hothead didn't try, just to get off a shot at Gregg. He was by far the most hated man in Riley for refusing to even consider running a retraction to the editorial.

Everybody who was anybody had called on Gregg at his hotel, in his office, at Ryan's bar, or they just stopped him on the street, trying to convince him to run a retraction. You'd think the whole Territory of Wyoming was going to sink in a big hole if he didn't publish it and send copies straight to the White House.

Even Sheriff Richie had said more trouble was coming if he didn't write it. "There's gonna be a war in this town if you don't stop being stubborn," the sheriff had said.

Gregg had listened patiently to most of them. But he lost his temper with the sheriff. His teeth gnashed as he spoke to him: "If Kassner has enough money and power to bend everybody in this Territory to his way of looking at things, that's fine with me. That's between the people of the Territory and Felix Kassner. But as long as I'm editor of the Riley *Gazette* and as long as I'm my uncle's nephew and as long as I'm convinced as I am right now that Felix Kassner caused the death of Flem Martin—I'm gonna call that son of a bitch in my newspaper! If that means trouble, so be it! If it causes you trouble, so be it! If it starts a war, so be it! That's the way it's gonna be! Now do you understand that, sheriff?"

"I guess that's about as clear as a man could be," replied the sheriff, rubbing his jaw.

Gregg had felt like exploding with several of the men who visited him, particularly those who dropped hints they would take their printing business to Bensenville and never put an ad in his paper if he didn't run a retraction. But he had restrained himself. They weren't worth his energies. Sheriff Richie was.

It would be good to get away from it all for an afternoon, with Belle and Dora and Case. They'd have a few hours of nothing but wide open spaces and clear skies. It would feel good to lie in cool grass and watch fluffy white clouds float by and have nothing more important to worry about than the possibility of varmints getting in the picnic basket, or a sudden rain squall.

Gregg hitched Skala to his wagon and had her prance down the middle of Main Street until he turned up to Belle's house. He carried the picnic basket in full view, and had Dora hold the blanket on her lap where everybody could see it as they rode out of town.

"You just want to defy them, don't you?" said Belle. "You want to show one and all that Gregg Martin isn't giving in to pressure, that he's packed a lunch and is having a picnic instead."

Gregg grinned. "You guessed it."

They went south of town for a couple of miles, then turned off the main road and headed for a clump of trees. Just beyond the trees was a grassy spot, hidden from the road, with a clear view of the grayish-purple mountains—and the clear blue sky.

They had no sooner spread out the blanket and opened the basket of food than Case joined them.

"Sheriff asked about you," he said.

"What does he want?"

"Wants to talk to you."

"We talked yesterday."

"About something else this time."

"What?"

Case shrugged. "He didn't say."

"Does that mean you told him where I'd be?"

Case nodded.

"I told you I didn't want no—"

"I know you did. Is that chicken in that bowl there?"

Belle took a bowl of pieces of fried chicken out of the basket and handed it to Case. "Help yourself," she said.

"He wants me to do what everybody else wants me to do!" shouted Gregg. "I don't want to talk about it any more."

"It ain't newspapering he wants to talk about. Besides, I think you took him wrong."

"I didn't take him wrong."

"He just wants to keep peace, that's all. He's not like the others."

"It comes to the same thing!"

"No it don't."

Gregg looked at Belle and then at Dora. "If he comes out here trying to get me to change my stand on Kassner, I don't want either one of you to offer him any chicken, understand?"

Belle looked offended. "It's not exactly your chicken, you know!"

"Please. I said please."

"I didn't hear you. You sounded like Kassner there for a minute, shouting orders."

"I meant to say please. Please don't offer him any of your chicken."

"We don't have enough to feed the whole town anyhow," said Belle.

They had biscuits and corn on the cob and cold potatoes cut into cubes. Case had a bottle of red wine. For dessert there was an apple pie.

Afterwards they all lay on their backs and watched the clouds roll by. Case got up to stretch and walked toward the woods. Dora ran to join him.

"I know what you're doing," she said. "You're looking out."

Case smiled. "Looking out for what?"

"For anybody that might come after Gregg."

He ran a hand through her hair. "You're a bright kid. Come on." They walked into the woods a little piece, then stopped and watched.

Gregg relaxed completely in Belle's lap. He was so comfortable it would have taken a herd of stampeding steers to make him move an inch. "The food was great," he said.

"It always tastes better on a picnic."

He opened his eyes and looked into her face. It seemed to float in the clouds. He pulled her face toward him. Their lips touched lightly. "You know what I'd like to do right now?"

"Yes, but we're not going to."

"What if we were alone?"

She tilted his head out of her lap onto the ground, then stared down at him furiously. He sat up, staring back. "All right!" he shouted. "Let's get it all out on the table!"

"I don't take lightly to being rejected in favor of a card game in a saloon!" she said bitterly between clenched teeth.

"A card game? Case and I damn near got our brains blown out!"

"Then why didn't you tell me?"

"It wouldn't have changed a damn thing!"

"The hell it wouldn't! I—I had practically offered myself to you. The least you could have done was explain why—"

"I didn't want you to worry."

"Bullshit!"

He paused, letting his voice become very soft. "It happens to be the truth, Belle."

"What makes you think I would have worried?"

He leaned over and kissed her again, lightly. "I just knew," he whispered. "And don't deny it."

He kissed her again, this time touching her breast softly. Her breath caught in her throat. She moved his hand, but not immediately. When their lips parted the icy stare was gone, replaced by a warm smile.

"If you ever reject me again, Gregg Martin—I'll kill you!"

Gregg smiled. Things were definitely looking up.

Sheriff Richie arrived about the time Case and Dora rejoined the picnic. "What kept ya?" asked Case.

"I had to double back a time or two. There's people looking for Gregg who figured I'd lead 'em to him."

"Much obliged," said Gregg, not budging from Belle's lap.

"I hear Kassner's signing up a small army," said the sheriff. "I don't know exactly what he aims to do with it—but there's men drifting toward his place from all over the Territory. The word is he only wants fast guns."

Gregg sat up. "Whata ya make of it?"

"I think he aims to take your paper, maybe the whole town. Not much to stop him if he does. I couldn't raise a posse big enough to stop him alone, much less a mess a fast guns."

"What do you suggest, sheriff?"

The sheriff grinned sheepishly. "I already suggested and you climbed down my throat like a bobcat."

"Where do you stand?"

The sheriff shrugged. "I didn't figure you'd have to ask that, Gregg. I stand for keeping the peace, same place I've always stood. If keeping peace means asking you to write a retraction, I'll ask you to write a retraction. If keeping the peace means shooting, I'll do some shooting."

"Who you figure you got to help you?"

The sheriff looked at Case and then at Gregg. "You're looking at it. Harry Pratt might pitch in, and your men at the *Gazette.*su01"

"How about your deputy?"

"I talked to Floyd just before I left town. He's going to run for sheriff after I step down. He figures he wouldn't stand a chance if folks knew he sided against Kassner in this."

"He's probably right."

"He said he'd do anything he could behind the scenes, where he ain't seen."

"You can bet Kassner's already figured out who he's up against."

The sheriff had a worried look. "This looks to me like the closest thing to a war I've ever gotten tangled in. I know a little something about locking up drunks and cooling off hotheaded cowboys. But I don't know nothing about a war."

"Most wars are started by the rich and fought by the poor," said Gregg. "I swore I'd never get involved in another one."

"It looks like you got no choice," said Case. "Unless you wanta turn tail."

The sheriff looked at Gregg. "We'll do whatever you say, Gregg. But you gotta lay out the strategy. You're the only one here that's fought in a war."

Gregg rubbed his jaw and stabbed the ground with a twig. "The way I figure it, he's got two ways to come after us. He can send his men in shooting and terrorize the whole town, or he can send 'em in a couple at a time and get the drop on each of us. He'd be a fool to come shooting. No need for it."

"Maybe that's why he's only looking for fast guns," said the sheriff. "He wants to make sure they get the drop on us."

"Maybe."

Dora's eyes became wide with excitement as she listened to Gregg lay out his plans. Belle looked at her with alarm, then took her hand. It was cold and it trembled at Belle's touch. Belle took her to one side, out of earshot. "You're letting yourself get too stirred up over this," she said.

"I—I can't help it," replied Dora. Her entire body began to tremble. "I keep seeing Bert Tyson leading those gunmen into town and I—"

"Stop that! You get Bert Tyson out of your head, Dora."

"I can't! I don't guess I'll ever get him out of my head, not as long as—"

"You heard the sheriff, and Harry Pratt too. Your mom's staying with him because she wants to stay."

Dora's eyes became hard. "She's staying because she figures she's got no choice!"

"Stop thinking about it, Dora. You'll drive yourself crazy."

Belle went to the wagon and got Gregg's poncho. "Put this on," she said.

"I'm not cold!"

"You feel cold. Your entire body is trembling."

Dora allowed Belle to pull the poncho over her head. She stuck three fingers through the hole in the front, where Gregg had fired his derringer. Her body stopped trembling, but her eyes continued wide with excitement. "There has to be something I can do," she said.

"I know how you feel," replied Belle. "But there's nothing. There's nothing either one of us can do. Get it out of your head."

Dora's eyes remained wide. She wasn't getting it out of her head, any more than she was getting her intense hatred of Bert Tyson out of her head.

She and Belle rejoined the men, sitting quietly to one side.

"You aren't giving us a hell of a lot to hope for," said the sheriff.

Gregg nodded. "The odds aren't good. We'll be outnumbered They'll set the time and the place. That don't leave us a hell of a lot to hope for. But if we keep spread out, keep alert, and concentrate on acting the instant they make a mistake, we might just get lucky."

Case shook his head. "If they get us lined up, like you figure they will, and they get the drop on us, it seems to me we need more than just a mistake on their part." He paused, then added: "It seems to me we need some kind of distraction, like when Millie screamed that time. You said it threw Jamie off.''

Gregg chuckled. ''Millie can't scream loud enough to freeze up all of Main Street.''

''I know, but if we could count on some distraction like that—something to throw 'em off for just that fraction of a second it takes.''

''You got something in mind?'' asked the sheriff.

Case shook his head. ''No.''

''Then we're back to what Gregg said, we just gotta stay alert and catch 'em in a mistake.''

The men nodded in agreement. Belle looked again in alarm at Dora whose eyes were still wide with excitement.

''Whatever you're thinking, get it out of your head,'' she whispered. ''There's nothing you can do, Dora—nothing!'' She felt like she was talking to herself.

''Just remember,'' said Gregg. ''When you draw, shoot. And when you shoot, kill. We can't afford any mistakes.''

Belle looked at Sheriff Richie. ''We have a few pieces of chicken left, sheriff,'' she offered.

''Yeah,'' smiled Gregg. ''Help yourself.''

''Don't mind if I do,'' said Sheriff Richie, picking up a drumstick.

Kassner looked like a dandy prancing around in his shiny holster. It wasn't a western holster, which automatically made Bert Tyson look at it with contempt. It was the kind officers wore in parades. The leather flap covering the gun butt was shined to a high luster, just like his boots. He'd been wearing it constantly for the past two days, since the men started straggling in.

He seemed to enjoy it, like he enjoyed this whole thing of playing soldier. He ordered the men to stand in a straight line while he marched back and forth in front of them, looking at their weapons and their horses, and occasionally at the men themselves. He kept Bert constantly at his side. Kassner didn't feel safe with those men unless Bert was with him.

They were worse than just a dirty bunch. They were filthy. Three had arrived half starved. Only two had brought extra clothes, six had bedrolls. The others slept where they fell at night. They stayed at the stables. The regular ranch hands balked at letting them in the bunkhouse.

"These men are as desperate a bunch as I've ever seen," said Bert. They were in Kassner's study, going over the final plans. Bert was anxious to get started. He wanted the job over with.

"We will dismiss them the minute this campaign is over," replied Kassner.

Bert grunted. "It won't be necessary to dismiss 'em. All we gotta do is pay 'em off, and they'll be gone like an ill wind."

"Nobody gets a penny until the job is done."

"They understand that."

"Do you have a full complement?"

"I would have if you'd let me keep the Indian."

"The man couldn't understand English!" protested Kassner.

"He understands guns."

"I don't want any man under my command that can't understand an order."

"That leaves us eleven men, one short of what you wanted."

Kassner had wanted two men to ride down Main Street with him. One on each side. He thought it would be more impressive if there were two. One would just have to do.

"Do they all know what to do?"

"They better. We've gone over it enough."

"Good. We ride in the morning."

Business in Riley crawled to a standstill as people stayed off the street unless they had urgent business. A few strolled down a boardwalk just to see and be seen. Something was going to happen. Everybody sensed it. Everybody dreaded it. Nobody wanted to get involved in it.

Case and Gregg practiced. Gregg wanted to add speed to his draw. Case practiced shooting the necks off empty bottles. The practice gave them more confidence and increased their powers of concentration. It also let off steam.

Harry Pratt cleaned the two sawed-off shotguns he kept under the counter, and borrowed a third one from the sheriff. No matter where he was behind the bar he was never more than a step or two from a weapon that was gleaming and deadly.

Sheriff Richie made his daily rounds as if nothing was happening. His casualness helped lessen the edginess everybody felt, but it didn't change anybody's thinking.

"What do you plan to do if there's trouble?" asked Theodore Bilkins nervously.

"I aim to keep the peace," replied the sheriff firmly. "Same as always."

Bilkins wasn't convinced. Nobody was.

Dora became more and more withdrawn. She seemed to have slipped into a fantasy world which she refused to share with anybody. Belle worried about it at first, then decided it wasn't unusual for a teen-age girl to slip off into a world of her own occasionally. It was better than living in the real world right then and fretting over the trouble everybody said was coming.

Belle refused to think about trouble in the future. She had a problem right now that occupied her thoughts. She was falling in love—an experience she didn't need right now, certainly not with a man like Gregg Martin. She had been in love before and she knew how it warped her vision, her judgment. If Gregg felt the same way she did they might drift straight into matrimony and Riley would be the end of the road for both of them. Is that what she wanted? Is that what either of them wanted?

No. She had places to go and things to do before she settled down with one man. No, damn it! No! No! No! She had to fight this!

She had told him with her smile, with her hesitation in removing his hand from her breast, that her wounded vanity was now healed and she was once again willing to submit, at the proper time and place. She would wait for him to make the next move.

And if he didn't? Then she would make the move herself. The love she felt had to be expressed.

But what if Gregg didn't feel the same way? He acted very warm on the picnic, but men frequently acted like that on picnics. What if he relieved himself on her, then went to the saloon, in effect rejecting her for the company of men? Or even worse, what if he preferred another woman to relieve himself on?

Happy and horrible thoughts alternately tumbled through Belle's mind in a crazy mixed-up pattern. She felt joy and then misery and then a confused mixture of both. Being in love did that to her. It jumbled her emotions, making it impossible to think straight.

Finally she gritted her teeth and squinted her eyes with firm determination. She would wait a reasonable length of time for him to call on her. If he didn't, she would call on him.

Her eyes narrowed into gleaming slits as she made her final decision: Woe be the bastard if he rejected her again!

CHAPTER 13

It was a beautiful summer morning. Years earlier, when Riley was first born as a railhead town filled with rumors of gold and peopled by hundreds filled with greed and hope, a morning like this would have made Riley hum with the activities of frenzied human beings. There would have been swearing drivers of six-mule teams, horsemen, pedestrians, sidewalk auctions of all sorts of merchandise; horses, mine stock, brass watches, blankets, dressed pork carcasses—you name it.

In those days immigrants from the plains rubbed shoulders with pigtailed Chinese shuffling under yokes hanging from their shoulders. Mexican vaqueros with silvered saddles, Germans smoking long pipes, miners in ragged coats, drifters covered with trail dust, saloon keepers by the dozen, harlots; they all mingled, traded, fought, loved—and died in Riley.

No more. Those days were gone. The boom was over and Riley had become another sleepy little western town, peaceful and quiet. Nothing much happened. Nothing ever changed.

The morning began more peaceful than usual. It was so quiet the dogs that usually frolicked in the alley behind Ryan's saloon remained under porches, sensing something unusual was about to happen, something big.

Harry Pratt opened the saloon earlier than usual, which he always did when Dora came to help him clean up. He loved to have her around, for her company as well as for the work she did. When she offered to help him, which was about twice a week, he started early so she could do her work and leave before the drunks started coming in. Harry didn't like for Dora to be around the town drunks, harmless though they were. He didn't like for her to have to see them.

He finished sweeping while she washed glasses, then he took the broom to the backroom where he kept it. When he came back all the glasses were clean, the wicks were trimmed, and Dora had gone. She usually waited until he told her there wasn't any more for her to do. Today she decided it for herself, and left without even a good-bye. Harry shook his head, smiling. She had a mind of her own, that girl.

He looked out the front window as Sheriff Richie walked by, right in the middle of the street. The sheriff was looking up at Bald Mountain again. It seemed to Harry the sheriff had spent most of the past two days in the middle of the street, where he had the clearest view of Bald Mountain. Harry waved, but the sheriff wasn't looking his way.

Harry opened the front doors, and left them open. No sense keeping stale air inside on a day like this. He breathed deep, feeling good in spite of the tension in the air, in spite of poor business, in spite of everything.

Gregg Martin got to the Gazette building later than usual. Since the new printer had been hired on, he didn't have to do much himself.

Bellevue was standing at the type case, type stick in hand. Gregg wished he could be half as fast on the draw as Bellevue was setting type. A Sharp rifle leaned against the type case. Bellevue always kept a gun handy. Most newspaper people did.

The new man, Fred Dawson, was at the imposing stone making up a flyer for Tilton and McFarland, the San Francisco safemakers. He looked up and nodded when Gregg walked in. His Colt .44 was on the imposing stone, within easy reach.

Gregg looked at it, "You understand what's coming?"

Dawson nodded. "I ain't heard talk of nothing else since I was hired on."

"If you change your mind about staying I'll pay you off any time you want."

"Might as well park my gun here as anywhere," replied Dawson. "No such thing as a safe newspaper office."

"It'll be happening any time now."

Fred Dawson nodded and continued making up the flyer. It was the kind of job he liked. Tilton and Mc-Farland wanted a flyer that blasted their chief competition, the Lillie Lock Company. Fred had written just such a blast. "A single hammer blow will break a Lillie lock," it read. "The most skilled yeggs and outlaws couldn't bust into a Tilton and McFarland strongbox."

Case Anders came out of the hotel, looked at the clear sky and went back inside for a chair. The hotel had a long porch, running the full width of the building. Millie didn't like to leave chairs outside, even in the summer, but she kept porch chairs lining the lobby wall for anybody who wanted to carry one out.

Case got a table too, and sat down with a deck of cards. He sat looking toward the street, toward Ryan's saloon, and the sheriff's office. He couldn't see the Gazette building. It was on the same side of the street and farther down.

Case was getting tired of making sure the four of them stayed in separate places all the time. He wanted to go to Ryan's saloon for a drink, or a few hands of cards. It wouldn't be so bad today though, with the weather pretty like it was. Somebody would probably join him on the porch of the hotel for a few hands.

He walked to the edge of the porch and glanced up to Bald Mountain. Floyd Hammer, a deputy sheriff, should be up there by now.

Bert Tyson rode almost even with Kassner, partly to be able to hear anything Kassner might want to say—but mostly because Kassner got very nervous if Tyson wasn't close by at all times. The vain little man was already nervous enough, just knowing the eleven gunmen were behind him, and they were finally moving. Kassner liked to talk when he was nervous. If he had nothing to say he would create situations that he convinced himself needed to be discussed. Tyson's job was to listen or pretend to listen.

"It wouldn't surprise me if a delegation of townspeople didn't ride out to meet us," said Kassner nervously. "Sort of a welcoming party!"

Tyson was glad he didn't have to reply. He was convinced Kassner flowed from brilliant to insane at times.

The eleven riders were all decked out with guns and ammunition furnished by Kassner. Eight of them rode horses from Kassner's ranch. They rode silently in an irregular line behind Kassner and Tyson.

To them the job looked easy. They merely had to cover four men while Kassner dealt with some newspaper editor. They'd started out talking and joking among themselves, as if they were on their way to a night of drinking and carousing, which all of them were. They couldn't understand why Kassner was taking it all so seriously. Five men could do the job, easy. But nobody argued about taking eleven. If Kassner wanted to pay eleven men instead of five, that was fine with them.

The sun felt good on their backs. It made them feel clean. They didn't get a chance to feel clean very often.

Kassner kept up a steady stream of nervous chatter. "Your responsibilities will be increased substantially after I'm appointed governor," he said. "Of course, your salary will be increased accordingly."

Tyson was tired of saying "Yes, sir" and "No, sir." He sat back and just listened, or pretended to listen.

"The first thing I'll have to do is arrange for the construction of the governor's mansion," said Kassner. "I must get an architect from Europe. There are none in this country worthy of the task. Don't you agree?"

Bert didn't answer, which caused Kassner to look at him quickly, to see if something was wrong. Tyson was staring at the mountains, a worried look on his face.

"What are you staring at?"

"That smoke."

Kassner looked up. "What smoke?"

"Up there, on Bald Mountain."

Slight puffs of dark smoke rose regularly from the top of the mountain.

"Indians?" asked Kassner.

"Not in these parts."

"Who then?"

"They probably put a lookout up there."

"Martin?"

"Or the sheriff."

"The sheriff wouldn't dare join Martin!"

"The sheriff don't join nobody, Mr. Kassner. He just tries to keep the peace."

"Then why would he station a lookout on Bald Mountain?"

"To buy time. If that smoke is a signal, the sheriff knows we'll be there in a little more'n an hour. He can get ready."

Kassner looked very agitated. "You really think it's a signal?"

"I'd bet on it."

"That means they're planning to resist!"

"That's why we hired eleven guns, ain't it?"

"We hired eleven guns to show them the futility of resistance!"

"Maybe that's what you hired 'em for, but it's not why I gave 'em all those guns and ammunition."

Kassner's face flushed red. "What you're suggesting is preposterous! I've heard from a dozen reliable businessmen in Riley. All of them said there would be no resistance from anybody except Martin, Case Anders, some bartender that was a close friend of Flem Martin's, and the sheriff. They said his deputy wouldn't even get involved!"

"Those four could cause a lot of trouble, if they've a mind to."

"Against eleven hired gunmen? Plus the two of us?"

"Men sometimes get hardheaded, Mr. Kassner."

"They'd be fools to face the odds like this!"

"Only if they lose."

Sheriff Richie saw the smoke and ambled over to the hotel as if he was just patrolling the town. "Be about an hour, Case," he said.

Case Anders pulled out his pistol, broke the cylinder down, spun it a couple of times, then closed it and slid it back in his holster. "How many?" he asked.

"Thirteen in all."

"Unlucky number."

The sheriff chuckled. "For them or us?"

"We'll know soon enough."

A serious squint came to the sheriff's eyes. "Why you staying, Case? It isn't your fight. Nothing in it for you, nothing that I can see anyways. Why don't you just ride out, 'n save yer hide?"

"I thought about it."

"You still got time."

Case shook his head. "I'll play the hand out."

"We're not holding very good cards, Case."

"Sometimes a man has to bet on the outcome."

The sheriff crossed the street and went into Ryan's saloon.

"Thirteen of 'em, Harry, about an hour out."

Harry gritted his teeth and rubbed his bar with a damp cloth. "I'll be here."

"Why, Harry?"

"I got my reasons."

"Flem Martin was a nice oldtimer. Hell, I owe my last election to him. But that don't mean I feel obligated to get myself shot over what they did to him."

"It's not just Flem."

"Getting shot up ain't gonna bring Shelly back to town."

"I don't wanta talk about it, sheriff. I told Gregg and Case I'd be here. I aim to be here."

The sheriff turned to leave.

"How about us having one on the house," said Harry, reaching for a couple of glasses and a bottle.

"Maybe later, Harry." The sheriff reached in his pocket and pulled out a wad of black tobacco. "I'll have a chew with you though."

Harry poured a half a glass of whiskey, tipped it toward the sheriff. "Here's looking at ya," he said and downed it.

The sheriff stuffed his mouth with a wad of tobacco, then spit ten paces into a brass spittoon. "Take care, Harry. I'll be back for that drink."

Gregg was reading a proof sheet with Fred Dawson

when the sheriff walked in. "Can I have a private word with you, Gregg," said the sheriff.

"No need for that. Bellevue and Fred here know what's coming."

Richie looked from one to the other. "You plan to stick around?"

Bellevue and Fred Dawson both nodded.

"You might all change your minds when you hear the news," replied the sheriff. "There's thirteen of 'em, an hour out."

Bellevue took off a long ink-stained cotton smock and hung it over the end of his rifle. Fred Dawson put a proof sheet over his pistol. Both of them went back to work.

"Kassner's got hired guns, Gregg. We're no match for 'em!"

"Whata ya suggest I do, sheriff?"

"Get outa town a few days."

"Kassner would still be here when I got back."

"Then do what he asks. Hell, man, it beats getting shot, and getting everybody else shot!"

"Nobody's gotten shot yet."

"You're as stubborn as your uncle!!"

Kassner talked the entire way, going over his plans for an inaugural ball after he was appointed governor, listing the cities of Europe he planned to visit as a visiting head of state, describing pieces of furniture and art objects he planned to purchase for the governor's mansion. The closer they got to Riley the more nervous he became and the faster he talked. He wasn't at all pleased with Tyson's reaction to his running conversation. But it didn't stop him. He explained his position over and over, rationalizing the action he was taking, frowning if Bert Tyson failed to approve his every statement as soon as it was uttered.

"Nobody can ever accuse me of being unreasonable," he said. "I offered Flem Martin many times what his paper was worth, just to shut him up. I did it for the sake of the Territory. He was hurting the Territory, hurting the progress of Riley. Ask Theodore Bilkins, ask any businessman in Riley. They'll tell you. Flem Martin was a wart on the nose of progress. He had to be stopped!"

"No question about it," said Bert.

"It wasn't my fault those foolish men you hired bungled the job and there was gunplay. You know I never ordered anything like that. Isn't that true?"

"That's right, Mr. Kassner."

"And then that horrible editorial. That evil pack of outright lies! If I don't correct it, my appointment could be jeopardized. The future of the Territory is at stake. There must be a retraction, immediately! We must rush copies of it to Washington, so there will be no question in anybody's mind."

"It's gotta be done."

Kassner sat suddenly erect in his saddle. "It's for the future of the Territory, Mr. Tyson. It's for the people!"

"Sure it is, Mr. Kassner."

Gregg Martin was the only one who had served in a war, the only one who had seen men die on a large scale. Since everybody concerned was convinced that they were facing a major battle, similar to a battle in war, they relied on his advice. Gregg's final warning was etched clearly in the minds of Case, Harry, the two printers, and even Sheriff Richie.

"I don't care how many there are, there will be a moment when we can win if we act fast enough and sure enough. They will make a mistake. Men always do.

"Just remember, don't go for your gun until you're sure you can get it clear of your holsters. Only fools commit suicide. And when you go for it, shoot to kill."

Even Sheriff Richie had to admit it was good advice. Gregg Martin made it perfectly clear that he wasn't asking anybody to die for his cause. He was merely asking his friends to kill for it.

In the sheriff's office, Richie checked his guns, the one in the holster and the one he kept in his belt, as a backup. He emptied a box of cartridges in his pockets. His hands grew moist and sticky. He rubbed the palms down his pant legs.

At the hotel, Case shuffled a fresh deck of cards and dealt himself a hand of solitaire. He felt butterflies in his stomach. He'd been told actors felt like that just before going on stage.

Harry Pratt rechecked the shotguns under his counter. There was one missing, the shortest of the three, the one he'd borrowed from Sheriff Richie. At first he thought somebody had stolen it, but nobody ever went behind his counter. It couldn't have been stolen. Sheriff Richie must have taken it, he decided.

He got a pistol out of the cash drawer and put it where the missing shotgun had been.

It wasn't like the sheriff to take the gun without telling him. It wasn't like him at all. But it must have been him. Nobody else would dare go behind his counter, except Dora of course.

Kassner's original plan was to lead the men down Main Street, signaling for them to peel off at the various key locations—the hotel, the saloon, the sheriff's office, and finally—to wheel in behind him at the Gazette building. But just before entering town he changed his mind. Something Bert Tyson said made him think there was a possiblility of gunplay in spite of their superior strength. Felix Kassner wanted no part of gunplay.

He couldn't imagine anybody being so stupid as to challenge his hired guns. His men not only outnumbered the opposition, but they were experienced gunmen. However, he had learned not to expect the expected from men in the West. They did wild things at times, impractical things. Kassner was convinced they were only half civilized.

"Take charge," he said to Tyson, pulling his horse to one side. "Send a man after me when the town is secure."

Tyson was relieved. He had been afraid of Kassner's ability to lead an operation like this from the very beginning. He felt much better being in complete control.

Kassner sat stiffly in his saddle watching the men file past. He resented their indifference to him, the way they slouched in their saddles instead of snapping to attention as real soldiers would have done if their commanding officer was reviewing them. They were a motley looking bunch, typical of men in the West, as undisciplined as they were unwashed. He would never tolerate men like that in the Territorial Militia. His militiamen would wear brightly colored uniforms, designed in Europe, and ride the best mounts available. They would be clean and highly disciplined, and completely loyal to his every command. He, Felix Kassner, was going to civilize this savage land. It was his destiny to do so!

The men became very quiet as they approached Main Street. Tyson pulled up to give them last minute instructions. "Gather around, men," he commanded. "I don't want to have to shout my lungs out, and I want all of you to hear."

The eleven heavily armed riders circled close.

"If you men wanta get paid in hard cash instead of hot lead you'll use your heads and not your guns, unless you absolutely have to."

There was a round of muffled chuckles and snarls.

"We aren't interested in killing anybody. All we want to do is convince a newspaper editor to publish another paper, reflecting Mr. Kassner's point of view. That's all we want. Your job is just to see to it that nobody interferes with Mr. Kassner. If you have to use guns, use 'em. But if you don't, keep 'em in their holsters and save your ammunition. Anybody got any questions about that?"

One of the men with a grayish black beard and pockmarked cheeks grinned, looking around the circle. "You sure make more sense than that little dude we dropped off back there."

"Move out," said Bert, taking the lead position.

Bert Tyson didn't make the grand entrance that Kassner had envisioned making. He walked his horse slowly, slouching in the saddle, his eyes darting from one side of the deserted street to the other. Case Anders was the only person in full view, sitting on the front porch of the hotel, playing cards by himself, holding a fresh cigar at a jaunty angle in his mouth. Tyson would like to push that cigar down his throat— and would when he got the chance. Not today though. There was no need for any violence today, and he wanted none. He nodded toward Anders and two men peeled off, stopping their horses in front of the hotel. They dismounted and walked slowly toward the front porch.

Two more peeled off at the sheriff's office and two others went into Ryan's saloon.

Bert and the other five went to the Gazette building.

"Hey, Martin!" he shouted. "Come on out, or else we'll come in and get you."

Case Anders looked up from his cards as the two men approached. They separated and started to go on either side of him.

"That's about far enough," he said. "What's your business?"

"We got no business with you, Case, only with Gregg Martin."

"Then what are you doing here?"

"We just aim to see that you don't interfere, that's all. You keep right on playing cards and everything will be all right."

"You two stay in front of me," commanded Case.

Each of the two men held their hands out from the waist, looking tense and ready. "Just don't try nothing, Case."

Case looked across the street as Sheriff Richie came

out of his office behind two of the men. The sheriff carried a wooden chair that he sat on the boardwalk. He sat in it and tilted it back against the building. The two men stood in the street, next to the boardwalk, and watched him, much like the two were watching Case—ready to spring at the first sign of trouble.

"Pretty day for just sitting, ain't it, sheriff?" shouted Case.

"Sure is!" replied Richie.

Both looked relaxed. They weren't. They were looking for a mistake. So far they hadn't seen one.

Harry Pratt came out of the saloon with two men behind him. As soon as he got in the bright sunlight he squinted and held his hand over his eyes. "That stuff'll kill ya!" he complained. "Why don't we go inside and drink till this is over?"

One of the gunmen looked at the other and smiled. "This bartender talks sense," he said. The three of them went back inside the saloon and Harry went behind the bar. He put out glasses and a fresh bottle. "It's on the house, gentlemen," he said, smiling.

As soon as Gregg Martin stepped out the front door of the Gazette building, two of Tyson's men darted inside to stand near Bellevue and Fred Dawson. Dawson shrugged helplessly. "Hell, man, we just work here," he said. Bellevue continued setting type.

Outside, Bert nodded to the remaining three men, two of whom walked their horses off in opposite directions, stopping in the middle of the street at each end of town. Anybody coming or going would have to pass one or the other. The third man galloped back to get Kassner.

Tyson looked distastefully at Gregg Martin. "You've gotten a little too big for your britches," he snarled. "We might just have to take you down a notch."

"Looks like you brought enough men for it."

"Mr. Kassner believes in doing a job right."

Kassner walked his horse up Main Street much like he imagined Napoleon would have done it, feeling eyes from the silent buildings staring at him. His lone bodyguard trailed dutifully. He pulled up to the right of Bert Tyson. The bodyguard pulled up to his right.

Kassner began as if reading an official proclamation. "I have prepared an editorial which I wish to see published on the front page of the next issue of the Riley *Gazette*," he announced. "It is my wish that the next issue be prepared today and printed in time to send copies East on tomorrow's train."

Kassner had a high-pitched, authoritative voice that had a mesmerizing effect on his audience. Nobody noticed the lone figure walking with a slight stoop until she had crossed Main Street and was walking down the boardwalk toward the Gazette building. She had a wide hat that fit square on her head, shadowing her face completely. She wore a dull-colored poncho, two sizes too large. There was a gaping hole in the front of it which she held together with her hand.

She walked with her eyes down. The gunman at the end of the street waved to catch her attention, but she either didn't see him or chose to ignore him. He hesitated, then decided to let her go. It was just a rather plain-looking young girl. No sense causing trouble over that. Case couldn't see her from the hotel, but he saw the sheriff stand, and grow tense. He looked over his cards at the two men guarding him and felt his blood begin to race.

Harry Pratt poured two more drinks, oblivious of anything happening outside. "I think I'll take a look and see how they're doing out there," said one of the gunmen. "You keep an eye on the bartender." He walked toward the window, his hand near his holster.

Bellevue and Fred Dawson continued quietly at work, ignoring the two gunmen who watched their every move.

Gregg was in the middle of the boardwalk, standing alone, looking up at Felix Kassner. Kassner was on horseback, making his official demand for the next edition of the paper. To Kassner's left was Bert Tyson. A gunman was to Kassner's right.

Dora stepped off the boardwalk just before getting to the Gazette building. She appeared to prefer to walk around the men rather than pass Gregg on the boardwalk and possibly interrupt their business. She walked around the three horses, then turned back in toward the boardwalk. As soon as she was even with Bert Tyson she stopped and turned toward him. She looked up into his eyes. Tyson looked mildly puzzled at first. Then, suddenly, he looked terrorstricken. He made a wild grab for his gun.

Dora's movements were steady and certain, as if she'd rehearsed them over and over until she now made them from habit. Her hand that had been clutching the gaping hole in the poncho was removed and a shotgun barrel was pushed through. It moved out only a few inches before it exploded, shooting a red flame almost to Bert Tyson's face.

The look of terror never left Tyson's eyes, as they received the full impact of the horrendous blast. His head was blown backwards with such a jerk his neck snapped. A second blast tore into his chest, physically blasting him out of his saddle. He fell against Kassner then bounced to the ground.

The two shots, coming less than a second apart, stunned the intruders, all of whom had thought the situation was well under control. The two guards at either end of Main Street stared in disbelief. Neither were close enough to get off a shot at Dora, even if they wanted to. Both hesitated, uncertain what to do.

The gunman who was looking out the window at Riley's bar couldn't believe his eyes, or his ears. "My Gawd!" he shouted. "She done blowed his head clean off!"

The second gunman rushed from the bar to the window to see what had happened. He never found out. His back was no sooner turned than a second set of shotgun blasts exploded from behind the bar. Both of the gunmen got blasts in the back of the head. The one that had been standing by the window was blown through the glass.

Sheriff Richie and Case Anders drew simultaneously, as if they had been expecting just such a diversion. Both fired four shots in rapid succession, then paused to see if there was any movement. Sheriff Richie fired two more shots, then pulled out his second pistol. Case didn't see any movement, other than muscle spasms, from either of the men who had been guarding him. He saved his ammo.

Inside the Gazette building Fred Dawson and Bellevue scooped up their weapons and started pulling triggers without pausing, aiming, or even looking.

"Gawddamn it, Fred!" screamed Bellevue. "You done got blood and bone all over my type case!"

Gregg Martin drew and fired pointblank into the face and then chest of the gunman beside Kassner, blasting him backward off his horse. He then aimed at Kassner. He had told the others over and over, don't hesitate, fire, and shoot to kill. It was the only way to win a war. Yet he hesitated. He was the only one of the four who did.

Kassner had a red line of blood coming down his forehead, and another coming from his left eye. Two buckshots aimed at Bert Tyson had gotten him. They were only flesh wounds. The one that lodged in his forehead would later be squeezed out like a ripe pimple. The other would be more difficult to remove. It had buried itself in Kassner's left eyeball and would only come out when the entire eyeball came out.

Gregg aimed his pistol at Kassner's head, but hesitated. Kassner stared straight ahead, in deep shock.

The gunmen at each end of Main Street came out of their stupor and made their moves. Each headed out of town as fast as their horses would take them.

Kassner turned his horse, his one good eye opened wide in shock, his other filling with blood. The horse headed out of town, at a slow walk.

Gregg holstered his gun. "Let 'em go!" he shouted. "His horse knows the way home."

Kassner sat erect in the saddle, like a victorious general—except for the red line of blood dripping down his forehead and the pool of blood overflowing from his left eye.

Riley became as still as a ghost town after Kassner

disappeared. Sheriff Richie was the first to stir, walking down the middle of Main Street toward the Gazette building where Gregg was holding Dora's trembling body. "You did what you had to do, Dora," he said softly. "You did it damn well too. Damn well." He looked at Gregg. "You better take her to Belle's house."

Harry Pratt came running out of the saloon. "I'll take her," he said. "I'll take her to her mother, where she belongs."

The sheriff looked at Harry's determined face. "You can't leave her at Kassner's ranch," he said.

"Who said anything about leaving her? I'm getting Shelly and bringing her back here—to my place, where she shoulda been all along."

"Better take my wagon to haul her stuff," said Gregg.

"Thanks," said Harry.

"I guess it'll be all right," agreed the sheriff. "I don't think Kassner has any more fight left in him."

"He better not," said Harry, holding up his shotgun. He'd already killed two men today. One more wouldn't make any difference.

Soon half the town had converged onto Main Street, staring at the bodies, asking each other questions. Nobody paid any attention as Case Anders walked by, carrying a leather grip. He went straight to the depot. "Afternoon train on time?" he asked.

"Near as ever," replied the ticket agent.

"One ticket to Cheyenne," said Case.

Sheriff Richie held a hasty conference with the coroner who obviously didn't like what Richie was saying. But he voiced no objections when Richie ordered a burial crew to get started on a line of graves and pine boxes to be made. "Move!" he shouted. "I want every body in the ground by sunset!"

There was to be one reading for all. He told the preachers to get together and decide which one did it.

"Can't we have a special service for Bert Tyson?" asked the minister selected for the mass funeral. "After all, everybody in town knew him."

"You can have any kind of ceremony you want," replied Richie. "Just so he's in the ground by sunset."

"It's barbaric!" mumbled a church leader, out of Richie's earshot.

Bellvue and Fred Dawson went back inside the Gazette building and continued setting type.

Belle ran to the livery stable where Dora was waiting for Harry Pratt to hitch up Gregg's Morgan. "Are you all right?" she asked, her eyes wide with fear for the child.

"I will be."

"Wouldn't you rather wait with me while Harry gets your mother?"

"No. The ride will do me good."

Belle stopped by the Gazette building to see Gregg Martin, just to satisfy herself he was all right. Too many people were milling around for them to talk. They smiled and nodded, then Belle left. Gregg watched her hesitate, as if she was going to turn around, perhaps to say something to him. He waited, hoping that would be the case. But she didn't turn. She resumed walking without even looking back.

Just the fact that she hesitated told him something

though. It told him he'd been a damn fool, waiting all this time to make his move. Well, he'd soon change that. Now that the trouble was over, there was nothing to keep him from calling on her.

That night every man in town jammed Ryan's saloon, all except Gregg. He had other plans, more exciting plans. He would take a hot bath, shave, put on a new shirt, borrow some flowers from Harry Pratt's flower box, and get a bottle of good whiskey. He'd walk in unannounced and before he left every button on her shirt was going to be swinging as free as a gate with no latch.

And later they would talk about the future. He knew she wasn't much for getting married right away, which was fine with him. He wasn't either. But they could still plan some things together. He wanted her to be a part of his future. He wanted it bad.

He reserved one of the two wooden tubs Millie kept scrubbed clean for trail-weary guests. Etta worked up a good sweat hauling pails of scalding water as he sat with a cigar, just soaking and anticipating. One of the big thrills a woman like Belle offered a man was the thrill of anticipation. He leaned back and closed his eyes, imagining those buttons flying loose in all directions while Etta picked up first one foot and then another, scrubbing them with a brush that felt like it had wire bristles. She used a bar of brown lye soap that chewed away dirt and grease like acid.

Etta didn't like getting her clothes wet. She took off her blouse to scrub his feet and back. When she leaned over the tub large brown nipples dangled inches from the surface of the water. Just looking at them excited Gregg's appetite.

When he got out of the tub Etta insisted on drying him, all of him. She was just as gentle with the towel as she had been rough with the scrub brush, making his body tingle with desire. He returned to his room wearing the towel around his waist and his hat. Etta followed, carrying his boots and dirty clothes, her blouse draped over her shoulders, gaping open.

Once in the room she dropped everything in the middle of the floor and looked at the bed with a frown. "Who made your bed this morning?" she demanded, staring at the foot of the bed that looked like the sheets had been stuffed in at the corners.

Etta had a passion for neat beds. She jerked loose the sheets and began remaking it, assuming the identical bent-over position that had excited Gregg the first time he'd seen her. He couldn't resist the temptation to reach over and pat her backside playfully. She wiggled approvingly, and continued making the bed.

Gregg looked down. "Oh Christ!" he said. Etta turned and laughed. The towel was sticking straight out in front of him, aimed right at her. She reached under it and squeezed. "My, my!" she exclaimed.

He later tried to think he was pushed, or perhaps pulled into the bed, but that wasn't how it happened at all. Etta was dropping her skirt when he fell on his back, on his own. And he offered no resistance as she straddled him on her knees, and carefully guided his cock between her legs.

She squatted on both feet and began riding up and down, grinding his cock deep inside her. Gregg couldn't have moved if he wanted to as she rode him up and down, taking pride in doing all the work herself. "Don't move," she said. "You just keep it hard.

I'll keep it happy!"

She rode faster and faster, finally throwing her head back and gasping in orgasm. But she didn't stop, not until she felt him come, completely and fully. Only then did she slump forward, completely spent, and rolled off.

Gregg suddenly remembered his plans for the evening and leaped out of bed. Just as he began buttoning his shirt Etta rolled over on her stomach, pointing her round bottom toward the ceiling. Gregg stared, spellbound. He'd never seen a more perfect ass. He dropped his shirt and straddled her on his knees.

He grabbed her waist and pulled her up until she was on all fours. "This time I'll do the work," he said, entering her dog fashion.

In a matter of seconds the entire room shook as the bed began to bounce. Etta stacked two pillows between her head and the headboard to keep from busting her skull as he drove his hard cock into her, deeper and harder and faster.

"Oh my God!" screamed Etta. "Oh my—" She buried her face in the pillow. She came with such a sudden scream the pillow only partially muffled it. Gregg didn't miss a beat or slow his action. He grabbed handfuls of buttocks and pulled her into him, driving forward at the same time. The smack of flesh against flesh was earshattering. He felt his knees weaken, but he didn't slow down, not until he exploded inside her, spewing his fluid in what felt like a stream that would never end, filling her, overflowing. His fingers dug into the soft flesh of her buttocks, pulling her to him for one last smack of flesh.

It was at that instant that the door opened—

quickly and wide. Belle's eyes opened like two full moons, her mouth fell grotesquely agap. She and Gregg stared at each other for what seemed like an eternity, an eternity of hell, each unable to move, to speak, to even breathe.

Gregg was on his knees, erect from his waist up, his hands clutching to Etta's smooth flesh. Etta's face was buried in pillows. He turned to face Belle, his eyes pleading. His limp cock slipped out of Etta and glistened from the light in the hallway.

Belle ran down the hall to the stairs, taking three steps at a time, stumbling, grasping the rail, darting across the lobby, thankful it was empty except for Millie sitting silently behind the front desk.

"Was that her?" asked Etta.

"That was her."

"Oh shit!"

There was nothing he could do. Nothing. It would be weeks, months maybe, before she would even speak to him—if then. Oh shit.

He opened the bottle of whiskey he had planned to share with Belle over a series of nightly meetings. He and Etta drank it all in little more than an hour.

In the middle of the night he was awakened by the nightmare of Belle's visit. He relived every second of it exactly as it had happened, from the sudden opening of the door to the shocked stare of recognition. Only this time the vision lasted longer than the reality. This time he studied the look of surprise, then anguish, then anger that clouded her eyes. This time he felt the torment of hell crawl over him in slow motion. This time he had time to notice little details he had overlooked in real life. There was one glaring detail that added salt to his painful wounds.

All of the buttons on her shirt were loose. Her nipples, like her eyes, seemed to stare at him in shocked disbelief, and then turn away in anger.

"Oh shit!" he moaned aloud. "Oh shit, oh shit!"

CHAPTER 14

A lot of people thought Riley would change after what became known as "The Killings." It didn't.

The afternoon train to Cheyenne kept leaving pretty near on time. The merchants kept sweeping the boardwalk daily, for the most part. Housewives kept pestering husbands to build them a freshly painted flower box, like the one Harry Pratt made for his bride, Shelly.

Felix Kassner left the Territory the day President Grant appointed his Assistant Secretary of War, Brigadier General John A. Campbell, as the first governor of the Territory of Wyoming. Most people, even Theodore Bilkins, were secretly glad to see him go. Felix Kassner had never made any friends in Riley and people felt uncomfortable around him. It's ironical that the last thing anybody heard about Kassner gave the town a good laugh, something Kassner had never given anybody when he lived there.

A New York newspaper pictured him as being an expert on the Wyoming Territory. "It is a country occupied by savages, both red and white," he said. In the same story the reporter said the patch Kassner had over his left eye was the result of a dueling accident.

Sheriff Richie got bored soon after the killings and turned his office over to his deputy, Floyd Hammer. He and Alvaro Cortes formed a partnership for bounty hunting. Cortes would track them and Richie would either capture or kill them. Just before he left town Richie made a special visit to the *Gazette.* "What are your plans, Gregg?" he asked, in a very businesslike tone.

"I think I'll give newspapering a try, for a while at least. Why?"

Richie looked very grave. "I want your promise that you'll let me know if you ever plan to sell out."

Gregg thought it an odd request. But he saw no harm in it. "Okay."

"They'll always know where to reach me at the sheriff's office."

Gregg nodded. "You interested in buying the *Gazette?*"

"Let's just say I'm interested." Which told Gregg nothing.

Dora Bensen was unusually quiet for months after the killings. She kept to herself and did a lot of reading or just staring into space. She was like that until Belle got her enrolled in a school for girls in San Francisco.

LaVida Tyson had provided the money. "We can't let this ruin the child's life," LaVida had said. "She's too bright and too pretty."

LaVida and Case both looked in on Dora from time to time. Case became a dealer on the Barbary Coast. A year after the killings he and LaVida married. Dora was a bridesmaid.

Etta's stepfather, Red Fred, came to town with the news that Etta's mother had died of pneumonia. He took Etta to Ryan's bar where they consoled each other over a bottle of cheap whiskey, then they made love in the stall Red Fred had rented for his horse. Early the next morning they left town.

Fred Dawson and Bellevue, the only ones who didn't have a personal interest in the killings, were each given an extra two weeks pay for damn near getting themselves killed. Neither printer had ever had as much as two weeks pay in their pockets at one time in their lives. After the saloon closed that night Harry Pratt had to carry both of them home.

The next afternoon Fred Dawson boarded the train for Cheyenne. Bellevue went back to the *Gazette.*

Belle Colburn got ready for another school year and worked extra hard with her various committees. She had plenty of time after she dropped all connections with the *Gazette,* and with Gregg Martin. He asked to call on her three different times, about a month apart. She refused to have anything to do with him. After four months she began to change her mind, but it was too late. Gregg didn't ask any more.

And then there was Gregg Martin . . .

CHAPTER 15

Gregg woke up one morning with one of the latest additions to Millie's staff, a plump redhead with a face full of freckles, rubbing her nose into his neck. He wanted to speak, but he couldn't remember her name. This bothered him. He concentrated a long moment, but it was no use. He just couldn't remember.

"I think it's time to go," he finally said.

"It's early!" she mumbled. "And I'm still sleepy."

"Not you, honey. Me." He rolled out of bed and quickly dressed, then headed downstairs for his morning coffee. In less than an hour his decision was made. This was the third time in less than a month he had woke up with a woman whose name he couldn't remember. It was time to move on.

He stopped by the sheriff's office to get Richie's latest address, then sent him a wire: *GAZETTE* UP FOR SALE.

That not only satisfied his promise to Richie, but it let the word out that he was looking for a buyer.

Gregg figured the Gazette building alone would command a good price. It was in good condition and in a prime business location. There wasn't a better equipped print shop for five hundred miles around. The Washington Press was the best of its kind, and practically new.

Gregg didn't have a firm price in mind. It depended on who was buying. If some politically ambitious investor bought it, somebody like Kassner, for example, the price would go as high as $15,000. But if somebody who wanted to publish a paper, an out-of-work reporter, or even a printer who wanted to plant roots, the price would come down to $6500. That's all he really needed. He wanted $500 down and he planned to carry the mortgage himself for the balance. If he charged six percent interest he would make $30 a month on interest payments alone. He figured he could live on that.

He wanted to roam the West, from Texas to California—from the Oregon Country to the Dakotas. He wanted to feel the dry summer heat of the desert and the cold winter winds in the mountains. He wanted to trap furs and pan for gold. The thought of getting a small string of cattle and even setting out a crop for a year or two appealed to him; as long as he was always free to pull up stakes and move on.

He felt he would always have that freedom if he had thirty dollars coming in each and every month.

He wasn't surprised when the town's leading

banker, Theodore Bilkins, was the first to make an offer. Bilkins had been looking for a business for his son for the past year. Gregg asked an even $9000. Bilkins offered an even $7000.

"I'm not bargaining," replied Gregg firmly.

"I'm making a cash offer!" replied Bilkins. "You best think it over."

That afternoon Gregg got a telegram from Richie: ARRIVE RILEY FRIDAY. MAKE NO DEALS UNTIL THEN.

Gregg met his train, anxiously wondering. "Where's Belle?" asked Richie.

"How the hell should I know? Now, about the *Gazette—*"

"Is she married?"

"Not that I've heard about. What the hell has she got to—"

Richie frowned. "It concerns Flem's will."

"Flem didn't leave any will!"

"Yes he did. We better find Belle so I can explain it to both of you at once."

Gregg was still shaking his head when they got to Belle's house. She too was curious, but not surprised when she learned Flem left a will. Nothing Flem did surprised her.

They sat in her living room. Richie very solemnly pulled out a long brown envelope which contained a single sheet of paper. Gregg and Belle immediately recognized it as copy paper Flem used when writing stories for the *Gazette.* They also recognized Flem's heavy, scrawling handwriting. Richie read aloud:

"Dear Sheriff: Wes Darby and I have been drinking a bit, but I am of sound mind and am perfectly serious as I write this. My nephew, Gregg Martin, came to town today. As you know I make up my mind quick about people, and rarely change it. There's no need to. I'm rarely wrong about people. I like the boy.

"As you know, I also like Belle Colburn. I want them to share my earthly possessions after I'm gone.

"In the event of my death Gregg Martin, my only living relative, should take over the *Gazette* as a natural and legal course of events. Belle should keep teaching and living in the house I loaned the school. If these two things happen, the will that follows is not to be made public. However, if Belle moves or threatens to marry anybody other than Gregg, or if said Gregg Martin puts the *Gazette* up for sale, lease, rent, or loan, this will is to be made public immediately.

"THE FOLLOWING IS MY LAST WILL AND TESTAMENT—All of my earthly possessions are to be jointly and equally owned by Gregg Martin and Belle Colburn, as long as one or both of them publish the Riley *Gazette* and manage the print shop. If they choose to sell, lease, rent, or loan editorial control over or production responsibilities for the Riley *Gazette*, all of my worldly possessions are to be sold at public auction and the proceeds of said sale donated to the charity of Harry Pratt's choice. Harry is the only man in Riley who understands what the word charity really means.

"Signed, Flem Martin. Witnessed by Wes Darby."

Richie looked solemn. Gregg looked confused. Belle bent over laughing. "The old devil kept it up right to the end, and beyond!" she exclaimed.

"Kept what up?" asked Gregg.

"Getting me married and getting you into the newspaper business."

Gregg turned to Richie. "Does he actually mean I can't sell the *Gazette*?"

"Not unless you want Harry Pratt to get the proceeds, for his favorite charity—which means free drinks every hour on the hour until all the money is spent."

"Some charity."

Belle couldn't stop laughing. "Every drunk in town will join in to build a memorial to Flem Martin—out of empty whiskey bottles!"

"Very funny." Gregg frowned as he visualized his monthly income slipping from his grasp.

"Let's not jump to any conclusions," cautioned Richie. "I think you should see a lawyer first and find out just how hog-tied Flem left you."

"What do you think of Brad Everetts?" asked Belle.

"Sharpest lawyer in town."

"I'll see him at the school board meeting tonight, and ask his advice."

Gregg nodded his agreement, then plodded back to the *Gazette* to see what kind of progress Bellevue was making with the next edition of the paper. He found the new man he had hired working on the few orders for ads they had received. Bellevue was nowhere in sight.

"He mumbled something about going to Bensenville," said the new printer, a young man who looked like he might stick around at least until the first snow.

Gregg finished putting the paper to bed, wondering what business Bellevue had in Bensenville. There were only four pages in this issue, with few ads.

Gregg, like his uncle, wasn't much at hustling business. But unlike his uncle, he didn't have a small group of loyal oldtimers who sent him ads whether he asked for them or not. As a result, the newspaper business was being subsidized by the printing business.

It was dark when Gregg stopped by Ryan's bar for his early evening pair of drinks. He watched Harry Pratt carefully, looking for some sign that he knew about the will. Seeing none, he concentrated on his drinks, then went to the hotel for dinner.

The next day he spent on the press, printing the *Gazette* and cussing Bellevue for pulling another of his periodic disappearing acts. When he stopped by Belle's house, late that afternoon, he was tired and cross. Her news didn't help.

"We're hog-tied worse than we thought," she said. "If we don't do as Flem says the house goes on the market too!"

"I thought he donated the house to the school."

"He loaned it to the school."

"So where does that leave you?"

"Looking for a cheap room, if you stop publishing the *Gazette.*"

"It must have stopped being funny. You aren't laughing."

"Flem!" shouted Belle. "If you can hear me, I hope you're burning in hell!"

"You're just making him laugh harder," said Gregg.

"What are we going to do, Gregg. I don't want to lose this house."

"We could try to bust the will."

"How?"

"With money. Hire attorneys, go to court, look for

loopholes.''

"Where would we get the money?''

"I'd pledge it from the proceeds of the sale of the *Gazette.*''

Belle paused, looking down. "Is that what you want to do?''

"No man has a right to dictate our lives from the grave.''

"I know, but—''

"Do you want to start paying rent, for a lesser place?''

"No.'' Belle paused again, avoiding his eyes. "Okay,'' she said in a voice so low Gregg wasn't sure he heard her.

"You mean you'll agree to busting it?''

She nodded, without speaking.

All the way back to the hotel Gregg kept seeing his uncle and Wes Darby reading that final editorial, laughing at every line, pausing frequently for a drink. He went to sleep with his uncle's laughing face looking at him, filling him with a horrible sense of guilt for planning to defy the old man's final wishes.

Early the next morning when he went down for his morning mug of coffee Belle was waiting in the lobby, looking like she hadn't slept in a week. "I can't do it, Gregg,'' she said. "He meant too much to me. I just can't bring myself to do it.''

Gregg felt a sense of relief. "It was a dumb idea,'' he said.

"He was a sly, manipulative old bastard. But he was my kind of bastard and—''

"I know what you mean. Come on, we'll have coffee and think of something else.''

Neither spoke through their first cup of coffee. Midway through their second Gregg's eyes suddenly lit up. "We can be a couple of sly, manipulative bastards too," he said. "Come on!"

They rushed to the Gazette building and to Gregg's relief found Bellevue had returned. He was setting ads. "Where'd the business come from?" asked Gregg.

"Bensenville," grinned Bellevue. "I damn near gave them away, but just wait until Riley businessmen see Bensenville advertising in their own paper. They'll be knocking our door down!"

"Very good!"

"Somebody better tend to business around here, or we won't have any!"

Belle had seen Bellevue do similar stunts with Flem. It seemed to make him happy. "We're here to discuss something more important than ads," she said pointedly.

Gregg led the way to his office, then waited until everybody was seated. "Flem made a will," he said to Bellevue. "He left me the paper and Belle the house—just as long as one of us publishes this paper and she doesn't invite anybody to move into the house with her but me."

Bellevue nodded. "Sounds like a pretty good arrangement to me."

"The problem is, I want to travel around awhile."

"And we don't want to marry," added Belle.

Bellevue looked at Gregg. "I gather from the look of you that you've figured a way around all this."

"Not exactly around it. His will stipulates that one of us run the paper in order for each of us to keep what he left us. I propose that Belle be named editor for a year, at the same wage you receive. I, as owner, will receive thirty dollars a month. Any profits above wages are to be divided equally among the three of us."

Belle pondered. "I'd have to quit teaching."

"Not necessarily. You'd be editor and publisher, but you'd delegate all of the printing responsibilities to Bellevue. All you'll have to do is write editorials and news copy—which you did for Flem before."

"I wouldn't want you around the shop too much anyhow," growled Bellevue.

"What happens at the end of the year?" asked Belle.

"We negotiate another arrangement. Maybe I'll be editor for a year, and you travel. Maybe we'll run it together and Bellevue travels. Maybe we say to hell with it and turn everything over to Harry Pratt."

Both Bellevue and Gregg stared at Belle. She looked down, chewing her lower lip, then looked at first one and then the other. "What the hell," she smiled. "Why not?"

"Looks like we made a deal!" Bellevue grinned.

Belle and Gregg spent more time together during the next three days than they had during the past year. Both went out of their way to be friendly, as if they felt silly for having spent almost a full year hardly speaking. But all of their talk was business; deadlines, ad rates, printing contracts, delivery schedules, wage rates for printers, and editorial policy. Belle became more and more confident she could not only manage the paper, but would enjoy it. Gregg never doubted for a moment that she and Bellevue would manage things better than either himself or his Uncle Flem. Both had a much better eye for business.

The night before he was to leave Riley Gregg paid her one last visit, determined to talk about things other than business. The first thing he noticed was her smile, warm and friendly. The second thing he noticed was her shirt, buttoned all the way to her chin.

"There's some personal things between us that need settling before I go," he said.

"Like what?"

Gregg took a deep breath and looked very serious. "I think I might be in love with you," he said.

"You think you might, eh?"

"Yeah, I think I might!"

"So?"

He looked stunned. "Doesn't that mean anything to you?"

"Sure! It means you think you might be in love with me. So what?"

"If you feel the same way I think we should do something about it."

"Like what?"

"What do couples usually do?"

"Get married."

"Other than that?"

"Go to bed."

Gregg grinned. "Funny you should bring that up."

Belle's eyes creased. "Gregg Martin, I'm not about to screw you for the first time the night before you leave town!"

He shrugged. "I could stay over an extra day or so I guess."

"Forget it!"

He frowned. "Damn it, Belle! We never will get things settled between us."

"It's settled. You're leaving for a year and I'm the editor of your paper."

"That's not what I mean and you know it. What do I come back to at the end of the year?"

"We'll just have to wait and see."

"That's not much assurance."

Belle chuckled. "Are you trying to tell me a good fuck will give you the assurance you need that I'll be here when you get back?"

"It would help."

"Your uncle's will should help more."

"You leave a man with nothing, Belle—absolutely nothing!"

She went to the hall closet and got a small package, brightly wrapped. He quickly tore it open. It was a pair of field glasses, gleaming new. "For traveling in big country," she said. "My going away present to you."

"You do leave a man with something after all. Thanks." He kissed her lips, lightly. She smelled clean and felt soft and warm. It was hard not to put both arms around her and make it a real kiss. Then he reached in his pocket and pulled out a gold necklace. He'd planned to put it on her himself, around her bare neck and watch it dangle between her bare breasts. Instead he merely handed it to her. "It should last a year," he smiled.

She kissed him, also lightly. Then she held up one finger. "Till next year," she said, smiling.

It wasn't the assurance he wanted, but he guessed it would have to do.

Early the next morning Gregg had his derringer under his shirt, his six shooter in his holster, and his rifle
lashed to the side of the wagon within easy reaching
distance. The field glasses Belle had given him were
on the seat beside him.

Skala was full of vinegar, eager to bust into a sprint
if Gregg gave the order. She pranced in a restless trot,
sensing they were beginning a long journey and eager
to get on with it. Gregg too was eager.

He was near the top of a rise when he heard the shotgun blast from behind. He lowered his head, simultaneously wheeling around and reaching for his rifle. On
the hill behind him was a lone horseman, ramming a
shotgun into a saddle holster. Gregg could barely
make out the outline of the rider. He thought it was a
woman, but he couldn't be sure. He picked up his new
glasses and carefully focused them.

There, big as life, was Belle, smiling and waving
good-bye with her forefinger straight up in the air.
Gregg waved back, slowly at first, then wildly after
she tugged on her shirt. He kept looking and waving
until Belle finally turned her horse and disappeared
back over the hill toward Riley.

Gregg snapped the reins, letting Skala gallop off
steam—for both of them. "Damn!" he shouted into
the wind blowing across his smiling face.

He closed his eyes and visualized Belle sitting tall in
that saddle, waving that one finger in the air, smiling
pretty. He wanted the picture clear in his mind. It's
the picture he would carry of her for a year, the one he
would see on lonely nights, the one he would carry
over lonely trails.

She was sitting tall, full of energy, fresh and soft and beautiful. The front of her shirt was open all the way down, exposing two full bare breasts; two joys that would be waiting when he returned. It was going to be a hell of a year.

And unless he screwed things up again it would be one hell of a homecoming too.

TENDERFOOT
Zane Grey

PRICE: $2.25   0-505-51813-9
CATEGORY: Western

Nobody wrote about the West like Zane Grey. Others have tried to capture the unique flavor of his stories, but no one has ever succeeded. Tenderfoot is the West as it really was—a time and place that have gone into legend.

FARGO #8 Valley of Skulls

John Benteen

The golden gun

A party of scientists digging around an ancient Mayan temple was trapped in the hottest corner of a bloody Mexican revolution. The country was crawling with bandits, the kind of men who would kill you for no more than an old pair of boots.

Fargo was hired to bring out the scientists, along with a beautiful woman and a legendary golden Spanish cannon.

PRICE: $1.95
0-505-51803-1

CATEGORY: Western

Springfield .45-70

John Reese

Price: $1.95 0-505-51789-2
Category: Western

Madman with a Mad Gun

Raitt was a killer with a big grudge against the world. Now he was out to get repaid for his suffering. First he'd kill rancher Mike Banterman and steal the payroll money. With his .45-70 he figured there'd be no stopping him. Power, women, money—his for the taking!

Day of the Scorpion
Gene Shelton

Price: $2.25 0-505-51787-6
Category: Western

The Hunter and the Hunted

The Apaches called him the Scorpion, and he was itching to show the vicious Henderson gang the deadly sting of revenge. The outlaws had raided his farm and murdered his wife. Now the Scorpion had to search the rocky desert for traces of the killers, knowing that he couldn't rest until his wife had been avenged and the last drop of blood had been shed.

Three Complete Western Novels:

Gun Brat
Wes Yancey

Breed Blood
Ben Jefferson

A Renegade Rides
Lee Floren

Price: $2.75 0-505-51788-4
Category: Western

Triple Western

Three action-packed, rip-roaring adventure classics, by three of the greatest Western writers ever to tame the wild frontier!

Fargo #9: The Sharpshooters
John Benteen

Price: $1.75 0-505-51790-6
Category: Western

One-Man Feud

The Canfield clan, thirty strong, had left their North Carolina mountains and were raising hell in Texas. When one of them killed a Texas Ranger, the lawmen sent Fargo in to root out the killer. The Rangers wanted no quarrel with the Canfields, but they figured Fargo was tough enough to hold his own against the entire clan.

HELLFIRE AT BRIMSTONE
By Jim Wilmeth

PRICE: $1.95   T51656
CATEGORY: Western

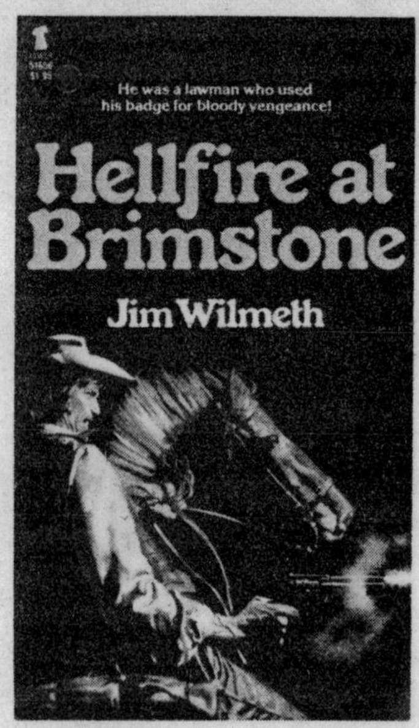

HE USED HIS BADGE FOR BLOODY VENGEANCE!

Lawman Luke Devlin and his brother Rafe rode out after the gang who murdered their father. In a badlands ambush, Rafe was killed, and Luke continued tracking. Through gunfights, fires and stampedes, the lawman knew he would settle for nothing less than a lot of blood!

CHASE A TALL SHADOW
By John Ell

PRICE: $1.95   T51655
CATEGORY: Western

HUNT FOR THE SHADOW!
Chamas, a white renegade who had been living with the Apaches, came out of hiding to kill two vicious marauders. Now he was the target of a massive desert manhunt, but first he had to kill the rest of the gang — one by one!